Mosquito Point

D1446346

by
Chris Barry

To Jerry –
Best wishes
Chris Barry

Royal Fireworks Press

Unionville, New York
Toronto, Ontario

Other Joe Bass Adventures

Mystery Creek
Sneathen & Gonne
White Wing

Copyright © 1996, R Fireworks Publishing Company, Ltd.
All Rights Reserved.

Royal Fireworks Press   Royal Fireworks Press
First Avenue   78 Biddeford Avenue
Unionville, NY 10988   Downsview, Ontario
(914) 726-4444   M3H 1K4 Canada
FAX: (914) 726-3824   FAX: (416) 633-3010

ISBN: 0-88092-318-0 Paperback
        0-88092-319-9 Library Binding

Printed in the United States of America using soy-based inks on acid-free
recycled paper by the Royal Fireworks Printing Co. of Unionville, New
York.

CHAPTER ONE

BILL COLLECTORS

It didn't bother old Jack the way it did me. But that's not unusual. IIe didn't care for old Andy anyway, although he was sorry about what had happened to his daughter. I had been fixing up Andy's house, in my spare time, because things were slow in my dad's house moving business, as well as at Jack's sawmill. Now Jack had decided he and I should try to help my dad by collecting some of his outstanding debts. That made me very uneasy. Jack is none too diplomatic, and messing around in my dad's affairs was not something I would ever even consider on my own. But that's not what bothered me most. It was this thing about Andy's daughter. Ever since I had heard about it, it was plaguing me. I wondered what the real story was. And, was my friend Leon's "Pop," as he called his grandfather, involved?

Here's how it started.

"There's an old fossil," Jack had said, "that's in a bad way due to the fact that parts of his house are tumbling down around him. He don't live far from you. He ain't got much of a bankroll to pay for repairs, so that's why I thought of you. You're clever, after a fashion, and ain't got a terrific overhead to think about." So I had gone down to see him. That's how I got involved.

Jack came aboard when the mystery surfaced. He's an old guy (though proud of the fact that Andy's older), who I got friendly with after he helped me through a couple of tight scrapes. He seems so gruff and unfriendly that people can't understand how I can get along with him, but if they knew better him, they'd see that he is really a pretty good guy. He does, though, have a little too much adventurousness in him sometimes. At least for my tastes.

Like I said, things were slow for my dad's business. A lot of new regulations had cut into his house moving. It was getting very expensive for people to move houses, and as a consequence many of them turned to other options. He had had to sell his big, new(ish) Mack truck that he'd been so proud of and fell back on the cantankerous "Old Pruneface," as we called his ancient (1953) Mack LJ. And he had one customer, in particular, who was really sticking it to him. Jack decided to make it his mission, using his "particl'r skills honed in my early, desp'rit days when I done bill collectin. Back in the Depression. Not real honorable. But I learned some neat tricks." He could concentrate on one thing at a time. I had to give him that. While my brain was swirling with a world of worries, not solving any, the old bird said, "Let's fasten on one, give it our best shot, then move along to problem number two. Now, yer old man's too much of a gentleman to put the squeeze on them Moultries in a pitiless enough way to shake the money loose, but if Jack Pugh is known for anything, it ain't his gentlemanliness. Them deadbeats won't even feel the razor goin' in their gut; they'll be too distracted by the finger poking in their eye. But when we're done, they'll know they been bled. And don't worry about your pop.

We'll put the money in his hand, and say Moultrie come up with it voluntary, in a moment of rare enlightenment."

Jack made it seem like it was all but done, except for picking up the money. So in spite of the queasy feeling it put in my stomach, I went along, telling myself it would be worth the trouble, since my dad really was kind of on his uppers and had had no success collecting himself. "That money belongs to yer dad," Jack said. "Them Moultries is no better than thieves. They must be dealt with accordingly, And with all the attendant stealth the situation requires. You're just a boy," he continued, "A snot-nose, as y'may say. Y' don't understand the value of a dollar earned but not received. Nor the deviousness and treachery of a professional deadbeat. I know, 'cause I been one. And with a certainty to Christ I know what works and what don't. I got a very effective tactic, and if it ain't been played on this character before, I guarantee results."

We knocked on the door. Mrs. Moultrie, the "brains of the operation" by Jack's estimation, opened it. Jack's appearance and delivery were by themselves very alarming to her, I could tell. He had taken the trouble to "dress up," which, due to his technique, made him look even odder than usual. He wore a slightly stained short sleeve dress-shirt, a crepe-y looking purple polyester tie, and had his best work uniform chino's hiked up so that his belt was drawn in tightly just beneath his rib cage. He had on his big, black orthopedic Knapp shoes, which look especially comical compared to his skinny white ankles and saggy white socks, showing due to the hiked

3

up condition of his britches. He fixed Mrs. Moultrie with his squinty stare, and started in with his raspy, nasal tirade. He was missing his four upper and four lower front teeth, and this affected his speech, causing him to sort of spit and slobber on his "s" sounds in a Daffy Duck-like way when he got excited.

"You are an unlikely looking person to be looking after Joe Bass's accounts" Mrs. Moultrie was saying. "Are you sure you have authorization to represent his interests?"

"This is his boy, ain't he?" he responded, jerking a thumb over his shoulder towards me.

"I wouldn't know," she said.

"Well I would. Now, we ain't here to give you a bad time, m'am, 'spite of what you seem to suspect. We just gotta make some progress towards settling your account. Mr. Bass is loath to sic his lawyer on you—that might ruin your credit. But if you don't make *no* effort, he won't have no choice. Now I promised him I'd arrive at some satisfactory result, 'cause I don't want to see nobody's credit ruined neither."

"I'm sorry, Mr.?"

"Pugh. John Henry William Pugh. Jack Pugh. Jack."

"I'm sorry Mr. Henry, William, Jack, whatever. I'm not in a position to make any payments."

"Okay. Fine Ma'am. I understand. But I gotta come up with something. So I 'spect me and the boy here'll

4

go around 'mongst yer neighbors and take up a little collection. You get along alright with the neighbors I gather? I'm sure some of them'll chip in, give you a little help while yer havin' yer difficulties."

Mrs. Moultrie stood there in shock. Not a word. Jack retreated with a business-like wave, and we began to walk to the nearest house. I was in shock, too, a little. The Moultries had gotten into hot water when they'd sub-divided their property and sold off a lot, which turned out to be based on a suspicious survey. Further study by the buyer exposed the fact that Moultries' house was actually straddling a boundary line. The Moultries had previously sold most of the lots in the little development over the years, and as they got closer to their own house, it was clear they were selling a little less land than they claimed each time. A judge had decided they could repay the neighbors on either side by giving each a piece of their own large lot, and that would require them having their house moved 50 feet to one side to maintain the proper setbacks. From the start my father didn't want the job, but as I've said work was scarce. Now we headed to the nearest house across the little street.

I had no love for the Moultries, with their checks adorned with praying hands ("God, please don't let it bounce," my dad said, showing the down payment check to my mom), but this seemed like an awful nasty tactic.

"I see it ain't been tried on her before. But she's tough. In spite of almost losing control of her bowels when I sprung it on her, she didn't reach for the check book. See, she can't write an intentional rubber check

5

for more than $200, cause it's indictable. And I guess she didn't quite have the nerve to offer less than $200 on a $3,500 bill, so she's gutting it out."

You old so and so, I thought. But I had to admire his nerve.

Jack climbed the steps and tapped on the door. I glanced over at Mrs. Moultrie, who still stood on her stoop, motionless. A little girl answered Jack's knock. "Your mom home, sweetheart?" Jack's appearance brought a look of panic to the girl's face, and she ran to get her mother. While she was gone, Jack turned to me and said: "Our gal's gotta see an adult standing in the doorway to achieve the proper humiliation." When the girl's mother arrived at the door, Jack said "Mrs. Moultrie over there" and he gestured towards her broadly with his arm, so Mrs. Moultrie couldn't miss it, "is having some rust in her water pipes. Now I have a theory it's hard water. Have you noticed any rust in your water?"

"No, not especially." she said warily.

"I'm afeared it's happened since her house was moved," he said, pointing to where it had been, then to where it currently was. Then he held up his hand and rubbed his thumb and fingers together like you would to indicate money, and said "It's kinda gritty, sandy. Nothing, huh? Oh, well sorry to bother you." With that we left the puzzled woman, and Jack made an "Oh, well, we tried" gesture toward Mrs. Moultrie and shook his head "no" as we headed toward the next house.

Jack was saying "boy, she's tough," when Mrs. Moultrie hailed us, and motioned us to come back.

"Paydirt." Jack said. When we got to her door she went in and got her checkbook and slowly, painfully, wrote out a check for $3,500.

"*Please*, don't cash it 'til the 10th."

"Don't give it to me if it ain't no good," Jack said, snatching it from her.

"It's good. Just hold it 'til tomorrow."

"Done, fine, ma'am."

As you might guess, my dad was a little dubious when Jack handed him the check, but he never could have dreamed up how Jack got it, so when Jack said he'd just run across Moultrie, who owed him a favor, I guess it was pleasanter for Dad to believe him than to speculate.

Jack was right. It is better to concentrate on one obstacle and try to take care of it than to worry about everything, and convince yourself that there's no way to win. And that's how we eventually straightened out the mess with Leon's grandfather and old Andy Jackson and everybody. But I'm getting ahead of myself. To tell the story right I have to go back to before I met Andy and tell how it all started.

CHAPTER TWO

THE DEPRESSION TRACTOR

There was a farmer in South Seaville who wanted to subdivide his property in order to give each of his two kids a building lot. This subdividing was turning out to be my dad's main source of work. To have the proper set backs and all, one of the property lines had to go right through the center of an old garage. Most people would have just torn the old shack down, but the farmer's wife was particularly fond of it and wanted it moved onto their lot. The farmer, though, didn't want to spend the money. "I have already spent $3,000 on engineering and other fees just to give some land away. I'm not spending one more penny on it, " is how he put it. But his wife knew my mom, and between them they'd cooked up the idea of my dad getting an old Model-A tractor, known as a "Depression tractor," which was stored in the garage, in exchange for moving the building.

"I was kind of cool to the idea," my dad told me, "But I took a look, and it's real cute. Come along, son, and tell me what you think." So I went. I like machinery and all, but for some reason this didn't appeal to me. Maybe it was because I couldn't picture what it would be. But all that changed when my dad and I looked into the little windows in the garage. It was like an old hot-rod, or more like an old dune buggy. It had big back tires, with worn out tread and wooden spoke wheels. The hood was askew and you could see the little flat head engine, and the disc wheels on the front like you'd see on a small truck. It had a cowl with a steering wheel hooked to it, but no roof or doors or anything, just a little school bus seat on a wooden platform, and pedals and gearshifts coming out of the metal floor.

"She's prob'ly a long way from running, but if you'll help me move the building, you can make it your project—they're mighty simple, those old Model-A's, and it's a good way to improve your working knowledge of mechanics." I didn't' know what to say. Of course, I would have helped him anyway. He usually paid me when I helped him, but he often put it into my "college fund." He thought it was good for me to know about housemoving and mechanics and practical stuff, but he also wanted me to go to college "so I would have the choice not to break my back for a living," like he did. Sometimes he even discouraged me being too much of

a "motorhead"—he didn't approve of "hot rod" type magazines, which I sometimes like to look at. He liked to read and stuff, and I think he wished he'd had a chance to get an education beyond high school. Anyway, he said "this machine's part of history."

"They were big in the 40's and early 50's. The Depression was officially over, but they hadn't told the country folks yet. Only the richest farmers around here had bought tractors—they bought an Allis Chalmers brand new over at the Ludlam Farm in 1939, and it was the talk of the town. Most of the hard scrabblers had some version of the Depression tractor. I saw them made out of old Flints, Federals, REO's, and all manner of old cars and trucks, but the commonest was the Model-A Ford. Joady Robinson had a Model-T tractor, but it wasn't as easy to deal with as the Model-A."

The house the garage served was boarded up and full of old baskets and farm stuff, and nobody was around, so we picked open the old padlock on the door. We took some of the boxes off the old tractor and hooked a chain to it. All four tires were flat, but my dad's pick up pulled it out easily.

We had brought some air in a blow up tank. There was enough air in it to get the wrinkles out of the tires. We hooked up the little tow bar my dad had brought along and towed it gingerly home and parked it in front of the garage.

"We better go move that garage pronto," my dad said. "That contraption ain't paid for yet. Let's load up some jacks." We got them loaded up and Dad's small trailer hooked up to his pick up when the shop phone rang, and my dad picked it up. "It's old Jack," he said. "Make it quick."

"Lady luck is with us," Jack said. "Duke Thompson wants to rent the *White Wing* for two more months."

Oh, yeah. I better tell you about the *White Wing*. The *White Wing* was an old, dismasted, retired oyster schooner Jack and I had bought and fixed up to move a house on—with the help of my father. It was huge—70 feet by 22 feet—and the bulkheader Duke Thompson, who was rebuilding a bridge at Grassy Sound, had rented it from us to provide an extra work platform.

I said "good!" and told him how we had brought home the Depression tractor, and that we had to go move the garage right away to get it paid for.

The garage was a cinch to move. First, we swung the doors open and backed the trailer into it. Then we nailed two by tens to the studs lengthwise along the two side walls, about 18 inches off the ground. Then we got four bumper jacks, and by jacking the two by tens, raised it off its little low foundation, 'til the bottoms of the two by tens were 12 inches or so higher than the deck of the trailer.

Next we cut two two by tens to go crossways, reaching out to the siding, and nailed each end to a stud, up snug under the two lengthwise two by tens. We let the jacks down 'til the crossboards touched the trailer, then removed the jacks. Then we doubled up the cross pieces

11

with some slightly shorter two by tens to eliminate their tendency to roll, and we were on our way.

We drove on over to the farmer's house, about a mile away, and backed it in to where he'd put some little stakes in the ground.

"I thought it'd take a little longer 'n that" he said. "Ain't got the foundation ready yet. Jeeze, I should'a been able to do that myself," he added, looking at our rig. "But I guess maybe you housemovers just make it look easy, Bass."

"Where's your blocks?" my dad asked. "I see you got your footers poured."

"Yeah, pouring wet concrete ain't so hard. The guy that delivered it helped me get it level. I ain't quite got the block laying figgered out. Roger over at the lumberyard told me how many blocks I needed, though, and I got 'em in my truck."

"Back 'er in. Let's get 'er done." We shifted around with the trailer 'til the garage was directly over the footing. My dad had trowels and stuff in his truck toolboxes. I mixed up some mortar in a wheelbarrow, and in an hour we had all the blocks laid.

"They'll be set up enough tomorrow to hold the building. We'll put it down then." We unhitched the trailer, leaving the front on its jack, and drove home.

When we got near the house we saw Jack, putting around the yard in the tractor!

If he wasn't a sight, the skinny old bird hunched up over the wheel, with his dingy little baseball cap on backwards.

"An A-rattle's the simplest operatin' vee-hicle in the world. Cleaned the carb, fulla' shellack, which is what we call putrified, rotten gas, put some clean gas in the tank, brought along a set of points, brushed up the mag, and give her a crank. Yer lucky I had a hand crank, they're gettin scarce. Used to stock 'em over Christman's years ago. Now try to find one," Jack said.

"They used to stock buggy-whips, too, Jack," said my dad. Jack squinted at him.

"That's a fact, Bass." All the while the "A-Rattle" was idling, or I should say sputtering, away.

"I thought you might want to get your hands on the old buggy, but I didn't expect you this quick," I said.

"When there's an A-Rattle to be started, Jack Pugh's your man. Course, it don't come up too often nowadays." I could see that we weren't going to be calling it a Model-A any longer. Jack had blown up the tires all the way with my dad's compressor. We each took a turn driving it. It was really weird—when you let out the clutch it lurched forward and took off. It wasn't geared down as much as you would think. But that was with the regular four speed transmission. Jack showed me how it had another transmission hooked to the back of the main one, an ancient five speed Mack truck transmission. It was so old the gearshift had a little slot for the shift lever to go in for each gear.

13

"High gear's always direct," Jack said. "Except in overdrive trannies. That there Mack transmission's from the early '20's—just this side 'o' chain drive. Now, each gear you drop down from high in the back tranny reduces the gear ratio of the front tranny by the factor of the amount of reduction in the front one. So if the front one was in second gear, say, and the ratio of that gear was two to one, and the back one was in first, say, and that gear was five to one, then you multiply the first numbers and you git ten to one. Now that's mighty low. You followin the math, boy? She also has a model-T truck rear. Worm drive. Many a winch was made outta Model-T truck rears. Nothing steadier 'n a worm drive. Oops. Losing wind in yer front tires. Dry rot. Startin' to give. Well, tubes is cheap. So's bald 16-inch truck tires. Now them 10-24's in the back is a different matter. Oh, well, 'course they're the same's what goes on yer big Mack, Bass. Coupla played out snow treads is all we'll need. You boys ever seen a Depression tractor with a scoop shovel behind 'er? I've dug lots of cellars and ponds with one of them things. Feller on the shovel's gotta hold 'is handles like a man, but be ready to let go when the shovel hits a stump. See, the scoop shovel was designed for a horse. And a horse knows to stop when he hits a stump. In fact, he's *inclined* to stop when he hits a stump. But a tractor's got no such sensibility. Even the quickest witted tractor operator can't stop his tractor quick enough to keep that shovel from flying up. The relationship between the operator and the shovel man is almost invariably a strained one. We dug all the cellars for Gus Meerwald's huge chicken houses with a Model

14

A. What we call A-Rattle. We had two sets a sprained wrists and one busted elbow on that job alone ..."

"I think we've struck a subject Jack's comfortable with," my dad cut in. "I got a few things to do, though, son, so I'll leave you two. But take notes. Ol' Jack's a wealth of information."

When my dad left, Jack picked right up where he'd left off. I heard all kinds of Depression tractor adventures, was warned of how dangerous they could be—Jack told me in gruesome detail about two deaths—one caused when a boy he knew was weaving back and forth 'til he went too far and turned the tractor over, and how the wheel caught his head when it went over, and another where a guy was tugging a stump while on a steep incline and rolled right over backwards. (I'll spare you the details of his injuries.) You might say I was given a thorough history of the Depression tractor.

When he had finally exhausted the subject was when he brought up Andy Jackson. "Has to have his chicken coob torn down," he had said. "It's been condemned. I never much cared for him. But it's a shame that the first building condemned in the last forty years in your township has to belong to an old geezer who can barely walk. The old widda-women who checks up on 'im comes around to see my Bert, and asked her to ask me if I could pull it down with my truck. I took a look, and it's all growed over back there, and the ground is spongy. I don't think I could fit my flat-bed in there, nor even my winch truck. But this little A-Rattle might just do the trick."

CHAPTER THREE

ANDY JACKSON

He told me where Andy lived, which was in a little converted chicken coop in the end of South Dennis, what my dad calls "Fostertown." I rode down there on my bike. His place was between two other houses, where people lived whose names I knew, (one of whom was the "Widda-woman,") but I had always thought it was an out-building with a little chimney in it—it almost looked like it was part of the "widda woman's" property. I had no idea somebody lived there. I guess I'd never really thought about it.

I knocked on the door, and after a while a ghostly little bow-legged man in boxer shorts shuffled to the door. He had real pale eyes that had a vacant stare to them. He was really pale, and his skin looked waxy. He had a sparse, grown out crew cut, and you could see every bone in his face. I told him Jack—by way of Bert, by way of the "widda woman"—had told me about his "chicken coob" problem. He led me through the house and out the back, through a little lean-to, to the overgrown back yard, and pointed to the shed. It had a big, red "condemned" sticker on it. Beyond the shed the woods went back indefinitely, out into the vast "Great Cedar Swamp."

He was just as matter of fact as if we'd had an appointment. He walked ever so slowly, just kind of slid his feet, barely bending his knees. He had on his moth eaten boxer shorts, as I said, a grayish t-shirt, patterned socks (with a lot of moth holes) held up by sock garters elaborately strapped around his thin, veiny calves, and little plastic slippers that had cracks in the plastic with foam rubber coming out. He looked so sorry and pitiful and poor that I didn't know what to say when he said "How much to tear her down," in a tiny, hoarse voice. When I hesitated he said, "Oh, that's alright. You'd probably never come back anyway. It ain't much of a job. People always forgets me."

"Twenty bucks," I said. He nodded. Then he turned back toward the house. He stopped just inside the door of the lean-to and pointed to the rotten sills just inside. The roof line was sagging as a result. The bottom of the siding was also rotten.

"You do carpentry work? I used to. Cain't hardly open a can of beans now, though. I'll pay you to fix them sills." I scratched my head and said I'd think about it. "Let's worry about tearing down the chicken house first," he said. Then he shuffled in to his house, pulled open a little drawer, pulled out a twenty dollar bill, and handed it to me. I thanked him for the money and said I'd be back. He said he hoped so.

The next day when we went to set the garage down on its foundation, I told my dad about the Andy Jackson project. My dad recollected that the old bird had built skiffs years ago, but he thought he'd gone to a nursing home. He said I could give it a try, especially since I'd collected a deposit, but be careful.

17

When we got home I changed the oil in the A-Rattle, which probably hadn't been changed in 20 years, then I made up some sides for the little platform on the back, and loaded on some chains, a sledgehammer, an axe, a shovel, and some bars and other "implements of destruction," as my dad called them. I also had an idea about the old man's walls. I threw in some old two by fours and some other, wider "two by" scraps from Dad's lumber pile, and two of the bumper jacks we'd just taken out of my dad's pickup.

When I got to Andy's, he seemed surprised to see me. He was pretty tickled by the tractor and ambled out to take a look at it. I started with the sagging back wall of his house first, because I wanted to see about an idea I had. The floor of the lean-to was pretty solid, but it was almost as low as the ground outside, and dug out underneath. Dirt and brush were piled up against the wall on the outside. The first thing I did was shovel the dirt and junk away from the wall. Then I nailed a two by ten along the studs where the wall had sunk the lowest, high enough to catch good wood. Then I put a jack up against the two by 10 and started cranking. It came up like a miracle. The ceiling straightened out, the wall straightened out, the wracked, busted window straightened out. Old Andy's dim glazed eyes lit up with an amazing twinkle. "You wanna see ma tools?" he asked. "They might come in handy. He pulled back a curtain (made out of what looked like an old sail) that walled off half the back room. Along one wall were dozens of clamps, a whole bunch of wood planes, and about eight or nine hand saws hanging above a long heavy work bench that had a couple of vises on it. Along the other wall was a bench saw, a band saw, and all kinds of things like heavy sawhorses and blocks of wood. Hanging above them were what looked like wooden patterns of some sort.

"Look around," he said. "Use whatever you need." He opened up one of the drawers beneath the bench and it was full of all kinds of razor-sharp chisels. Another had spokeshaves and draw-knives, another had a drill and bits, yet another had all shapes and sizes of hammers, and so on down the line.

"I loaned out my portable electric saw, and never got it back. But you'll find them handsaws sharp enough for your jack studs." Below the bench on the floor was a whole row of boxes of nails—copper, bronze, galvanized—and all sorts of bolts and screws.

I took down one of the hand saws, and Andy said "you gonna cut down them rotten studs? Use the backsaw." He pointed to a funny, short, square looking saw that had a handle that came up off the top at an angle. I took it down and cut one of the studs off up

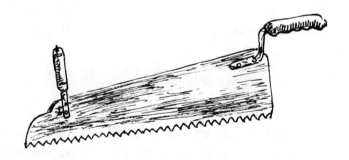

high enough to catch some good wood, and the saw worked like a charm. It fit neatly between the studs and you could use it without barking your knuckles. I cut off all the rotten studs in the stretch I'd jacked up, then got a regular crosscut saw and cut a new sill, leaving a space where the foot of the jack was to be filled in later, then cut some jack studs to scab onto the ones I'd shortened. I nailed the jack studs to the main studs, then toe-nailed the bottoms to the sills, and let off the pressure with the jack. I tore off the rotten pieces of clapboards, then went out and pulled a few decent ones that were left on the condemned chicken house. I nailed them in place, and that part of the wall was done.

"You made an old man very happy, son. That is a right smart trick. I built many and many a boat in my day, and I know a smart trick when I see one."

I went along and tackled another little sag in the wall, and Andy shuffled along after me.

"I don't know what you're gonna charge, but you're worth the money. Back when I was a-building boats, I wouldn'a let that dry rot creep up on me. But I been having mighty bouts with my joints. Don't feel too bad today. But some days it's all I can do to get out of my chair."

"You were a boat builder, huh?"

"Son," he said in his quiet, scratchy voice. "I done everything but fly an airplane and drive a locomotive. Teamster, telephone lineman, fisherman, rodeo, you name it. But yes, I banged together many a boat."

I paused and turned to face him, and as I did he said, "Son, how old do you think I am?" Now, I had misfired on this once before, when I was much younger, estimating an old woman's age at 100 when she'd asked that question. I remember the look that went across her face. So even though Andy looked older than Jack, (who was a well worn 75) by at least a decade, I thought a minute and said "uh, 63?" His face lit up again with that terrific twinkle, and he shook a little with laughter. "Son, would you believe I'm 80? I guess maybe I don't look as bad as I thought I did."

Of course I could believe it, but I felt I'd made up a little bit for that bad estimate I'd made years before. "You're kidding," I said. "I'd believe 65 maybe, tops."

"Son, you've made yourself a friend," Andy said. He commenced telling me all about the different boats he'd built or helped build. He had worked up at the Dorchester Ship Yard in the 1940's, building minesweepers and such for the government. He'd worked for Clem Troth and Carl Adams in the early 50's. But whenever he could, he built boats on his own. Even when he was a telephone lineman or fisherman, he fit in boatbuilding when he could.

"Troth built a fine boat. Sweetest designs you ever seen. Adams done alright, too. A little heavier built than the Troth, even, his boats were, and pretty. But all that round chine, fancy-fancy stuff takes a lot of time. So you gotta charge a lotta money. And of course they made big boats. I like a flattie or a deadrise. Simple, cheap, and very functional. I built boats up to 30 foot. But the best boat, and the one I stuck to when I got older, was

21

the flatiron type skiff. Sixteen foot was my most popular. In my later years, that's all I built. The 16-foot Fostertown skiff. Two men could easily carry her. She'd plane very handy with a 10 horse. Fly with a 20 or 25. And she'd chug along fine with a little four or five horser. I'd give her a little more rocker if a body was gonna use a little motor or row her. That means the bottom would curve up towards the surface running aft, or towards the back. That's the same with my sailing skiff. When I was a sprout, sailing garveys and flatties was the workhorses of the backbays. When motors became pop'lr, they kinda disappeared, but I made some in the '50s for a couple of the old salts. Daggerboard and spritsail rig, sometimes lateen. And they was fair fliers."

"But if you was gonna put some power to her I'd run her straight as a ruler. That's to keep her nose down. She'd jump right up on top and go like a jack rabbit. Now, unless you're going, say, 24 foot or bigger, you shouldn't oughtta spend too much time offshore, where things can get sloppy and stay that way. And if you're not goin't out there, if you're stayin in sheltered water, what do you need a boat bigger'n 16 foot for? How often you gonna take out more'n four or five people? My little skiff would handle that crowd fine. I see folks in a fiberglass boat, 16, 17 feet long, 50 horsepower outboard, 100 horse even. That burns a lotta sauce. You see, fiberglass ain't got no stiffness to it. So they gotta be built terrible heavy for their size. You'll burn 30-40 gallon a day roarin around in one. My boat, why, a six gallon tank you can run all day and most of tomorrow. She's quick. She's stable. Not too small. Not too big.

22

That's Andy Jackson's Fostertown skiff. But son, I made my last one a good while before you was born."

Now I was a particular fan of flatiron skiffs, too. They are so simple, in a way, but can be very graceful, when made right. I'd heard of the Fostertown skiff. Now I came to find out that here, right under my nose, was the guy who had made them. Right in this little chicken coop of a house, which from the outside didn't look big enough even for old Andy.

CHAPTER FOUR

VIRGINIA

That was the day I first heard of Virginia.

"There's a little old carcass of a boat," Andy said as I headed out to size up the condemned chicken coop, "that you'll find laying inside. If it ain't too broke down to move, could you, maybe, carry her out into the open so's I could glimpse her one last time? I was gonna try to pretend it wasn't there, but I can't." The coop was full of debris so rotten and beat by the elements that you could hardly tell what they'd been. You could recognize the laying boxes, and some of the stuff that had obviously been furniture, but now it was all just junk. The roof had holes in it you could throw a football through, and weeds grew below them where they could get a good supply of water and light. But down along the low back wall, after I had pulled out some of the junk, I saw the cutest looking little skiff you ever saw. It was about 15 foot, and low, and had decking over the front and back. It had a centerboard, and a couple of seats, and a mast step in the forward deck. Hanging from the rafters was a mast, boom, and sprit, fairly protected from the weather, though they were quite gray, with bits of thin, rotten rope hanging from the thimbles and pulleys. A rudder lay flat in the dirt, but was so rotten it just fell apart when I lifted it. The bottom of the boat had sort of "melted" into the dirt floor, so that when I lifted the bow up the centerboard trunk just stayed there, as if it had grown up out of the ground. I took the shell out with me. Some

24

of the bottom boards remained where the upswept bow had kept them above the earth floor, and with the transom and decking to hold things together I was able to bring the bottomless shell out into the open in one piece.

"That's Virginia's boat," Andy said quietly, and hoarsely. His pale eyes filled as he stood and gazed at it. I dragged out the mast and boom and all and laid them out beside it, to make the whole picture complete. Andy's gaze shifted up and out toward the deep forest that stretched far out behind his place.

"She could sail like Magellan, that girl. Sail right up Dennis Creek, neat as you please. All the curves and bends in that narrow ditch was just so much amusement to her. Almost never used her oars. I saved up and bought her a one and a half horse SeaKing outboard, so she could get back if she was in irons a way off from home, or against the tide, without having to row so far. She stashed that up under the bow deck. I worried for her being off on that big meadow, but she loved them birds, and couldn't get enough of trooping around after them up and down all them sluices and byways. And the way she could handle a boat would set your mind at ease.

"Them birds didn't hardly notice her, after a while, as she swept along so silent. And then one day, she didn't come back." His eyes filled up some more, and his voice was almost too quiet to hear when he said the last part. Little tears trickled down his sunken cheeks, and I didn't have the heart to move or say anything for a while.

Finally I tiptoed out front and started the old tractor, and drove on around back between the trees and stumps. Andy brightened up when he saw me, and he shuffled over to watch me hook a chain to the corner-post of the building, and from there to the back of the tractor. I tightened the chain by pulling ahead, then gave her a little juice. The tractor reared up a little, and I put in the clutch real quick, remembering Jack's horror stories. It was tougher than I thought, that old shack, and I had to rock forward and back to get the building shaking. It was post and beam, though, everything notched and pinned together, so when it finally gave the whole thing came down like a stack of dominoes. I salvaged all the good wood there was to use for fixing Andy's house. There wasn't too much. The rest I dragged out front to be loaded on Jack's old flatbed truck, so we could take it to the dump.

Jack brought down his truck from Delmont. It was a 1948 International Harvester with a flatbed that dumped, so it was ideal. He was a little grumpy about it, though. It took almost all day to load it, and we had it stacked sky high. When we got to the dump and were weighed in the dumping fee came to $68! I had the $20 from old Andy, and Jack, without much enthusiasm, wrote out a check for the rest.

"You're a fine young businessman. If I was to charge for the use of the truck, and my time, just think how far in the hole you'd be. But I guess I'll just deduct the $48 from your share of the rental of the schooner to Duke

Thompson. I'll eat my usual fee, and see if it don't apply to my merit badge."

Andy felt bad when he heard how much the dumping fee was. "I got a check coming on the 15th of the month," he said hopefully as he pulled out the "secret" drawer under his little kitchen table. "And here's thirty three 'til then. That don't account for the carpentry work, neither. Make me up a bill for that, and don't be shy, 'cause there's lots more to do, and a well paid carpenter is a carpenter who comes back, as I've always said."

I didn't have the heart to take his last $33, so I came up with an idea.

"Do you think you could help me build a skiff, if I get the lumber?"

He stood and considered, his eyes widening and narrowing. Then he said, "Son, I wish I could. But I'm s' blamed feeble I could never swing a hammer or push a plane. It takes considerable skill to do them things, and I can't just tell you how. I'd have to show you. But I can't."

"Good," I said. "When do we start?" He wasn't the first old geezer that told me something was impossible. "Give me an idea of the lumber we'll need, and we'll get started as soon as I'm done fixing your walls."

He looked a little bewildered, but after a while he said "git a piece of something to write on." And as the list started to come together, his eyes began to light up again.

CHAPTER FIVE

LEON'S HOUSE

That night I asked my dad if he remembered Virginia Jackson. He said, "Oh, yeah, I was just a boy at the time. I remember my older brother (my Uncle Otis) was taking me and yer grandmom a row on the creek about that time in his leaky little flatiron, and some fella he knew saw us there and said 'You out looking for Ginny Jackson?' and Otis said 'No, just taking the kid for a ride.' That is a very vivid memory for some reason. The whole trip I was afraid we'd find 'Ginny,' floating wrong side up and two days dead. But it was Pop Berman who actually found her. He had a little inboard Lyman. A new one. Tied up right there at old Ray's place, up close to the bridge. It was almost too much class for that Creek to handle. Anyway, he went out, fishing I think, and found her somewhere around Sluice Creek. They had found her boat the same day she'd turned up missing. Rudy Smick saw it, when he was out spraying DDT for the Mosquito Commission. Had the sails up and everything. She musta just slipped overboard. She was supposed to be a good swimmer, but it was fall, and the water was too cold to last very long in. Yessir, it caused quite a big stir at the time. Her mother died not long after—of a broken heart some said."

For some reason I couldn't get the episode out of my head. Especially since I had handled the skiff and all. I wanted to ask Andy if I could see a picture of her. I wondered what had really happened to her—how she'd come to fall overboard and all. I went over to my friend Leon's—Pop Berman is his grandfather. Leon's an orphan, so he lives with Pop, along with his grandmother and an old maiden aunt, who is her sister. It's a little spooky over there. They live in the biggest house anywhere around. It's a brick mansion almost, and old. Leon says it was built in 1801.

One time when a new cedar roof was being put on, Leon and I popped out through the rafters where some of the laths had been torn off to talk to the roofers. The workers, who weren't too much older than us, let us up on the roof, which was steep and scary. Oak laths, one inch by two inches and as hard as rock, were what the shingles were nailed into. It was like a slanted ladder. The roof was so steep you could never stand on it without ladder jacks where the new shingles were going on. Anyway, we were talking to them and watching them tear off old shingles, when one of the guys said, "hey, look at this old coin." It was right up on the rafter between some laths. He handed it to Leon, who wiped it off. It was an 1817 penny, as big as a half dollar and in excellent shape. Right near it they found a little whale bone nit comb, and they gave that to me. I must have been a place kids could have got at from the inside at one time, we figured. Then down inside the soffit the guy found a sledge hammer, in perfect shape, like it was just left there from banging in pegs, back in 1801. Leon said why didn't the roofer keep it, because they seemed so excited with it, and Leon wouldn't mention it to Pop, who already had tons of antiques.

Anyway, it was that kind of house. Three stories, in the main part, and all kinds of rooms, and a huge, beautiful staircase. My dad said Pop bought it for a song back in the Depression, when nobody could afford to fix the place up, or even heat it. But I don't really know what the price was. My dad never had anything good to say about Pop, and Pop was sort of snobby in a way, but he was the best of the three of those old geezers who looked after Leon, at least as far as how I got treated.

Leon's granny was the worst. My friend Freddy Chance had nicknamed her "Granny Grunt," because she kind of grunted at us and would sometimes smack us with a flyswatter. She would just look at us when we came to the door, while her sister would stand behind her and say "Leon's got a cold," or, if you were lucky, "wipe your feet," which meant you could come in, but they weren't thrilled about it.

So you can see why I always hesitated a little when I thought about going over there. But this Virginia thing was under my skin. The old gals didn't seem any more disappointed than usual to see me, and Leon was real pleased. We went down into the basement, which is really cool. It has all these brick girders and arches, and Pop has his big train set up down there, and Leon has some of his bigger stuff down there too. I went right to asking him about Virginia, but he had never heard of her. He was intrigued, though, and said he'd take it up with Pop. Just then Pop came downstairs, to mess with his trains, I guess. And he was in a pretty good mood. He said "How ya doin, sport?" and tousled my hair, like I was a little kid. But I didn't mind. I was just glad he wasn't there to send me packing, like he sometimes did.

Leon said "Pop, what do you know about Virginia Jackson? I heard something about it and it sounded pretty interesting. You were the one that found her, her body, I mean, weren't you?" As soon as he said the name, Pop looked over at me, and his smile vanished.

"Is somebody writing a book around here?" he said. Then, "I don't have anything to say about that right now." Then he left. And we both felt mighty uncomfortable.

CHAPTER SIX

JACK PITCHESIN

Next person I turned to was old Jack, since I didn't have the nerve yet to bring it up with Andy again. I had looked him up about sawing some oak for ribs for my boat project, and maybe the cedar for the planking, if I could skid some logs from out behind Andy's with the tractor. When I brought up the subject of Virginia's disappearance and Rudy Smick, Jack wasn't shy. But then, he never is.

"Oh, yeah. I done a little reconnaissance myself in the old Stearman. But I had to share airspace with that no good Rudy Smick. He's the one who spotted the empty boat. Always made me suspicious. He had no love for that Jackson girl. She was stirring up quite a little trouble over that DDT. And Rudy had the contract to spray it for the Skeeter Mission. I'd tried to get it, but he had the connections. I only had a 220 Continental motor on the Stearman then, and he had an N3N, with a 300 Lycoming. Very spiffy. You couldn't tell us apart from the ground, I expect, but his ship carried more stuff.

I ain't sorry, though. His wife got the cancer from cleaning out his clothes. Not old Rudy, though. Oh, he was the dashingest sort, or at least he thought so. He's the one who deserved the cancer, but he was too ornery. Now he calls hisself a 'batchelor,' like the old gal never existed. He hung up his wings, but he don't never let nobody forget he was a flyboy. Now all the old bats swarm him like flypaper. Used his charm and political connections to get himself one of them government jobs—oh, I don't know what it was, one of them jobs where your tasks is hard to define but easy to perform. Retired with any number of pensions—even one from the Skeeter Mission, I've heard. Plus he inherited the nice home his poor wife had inherited from *her* family, along with two others he swindled old widda women out of. That's Rudy Smick, and the less dealings you have with him, the safer your financial future is.

"Him and old Pop Berman was tight.—Pop sold chemicals for Dupont or one of them. Sold to the Skeeter Mission, and Rudy helped him there. I don't know how many different ways the kickbacks went, but it was on the advanced math level. Pop and him had some kind of falling out, though. I don't know what it was. The Jackson girl was raising a terrible ruckus over the DDT, like I say, and the Skeeter Mission, and Pop, Rudy and the boys from the chemical companies were none too pleased. They tell me she'd bring all kinds of dead birds, fish, and muskrats and God knows what and all down to the monthly meetings of the Commission. Told them the DDT done it. We all thought it was harmless at the time. But I begun to have my doubts, and that's when I moved

33

from crop dustin' to crop duster repair, and then out of it altogether. My Bert was the one who first raised a fuss with me. She seen a lot of birds and stuff bite the dust when I sprayed, and she wouldn't let none of the stuff around the house near the kids. Made a perfect nuisance of herself. But all in all, looking back, I expect she was right about that one.

"Anyhow, that's about the time Pop and Rudy fell out. When the girl died. I can't believe that Pop got a conscience all of a sudden, but maybe he was scared, because he quit selling the chemicals. It was a sideline, anyway. And him and Smick wasn't bosom pals no more. I never thought a whole lot about it, but it is a might strange when you come to think on it, as if that girl's death figured into it some way. Maybe we oughtta ask Jackson about it." Then I knew he was hooked, too.

CHAPTER SEVEN

MATERIALS

"Got yer cedar, boy?" Andy asked when I showed up to finish shoring up his saggy, drafty back wall.

"I'm gonna go out back of here and see if I can spot a few nice trees." I said. "You think anybody will notice?"

"Help yourself, boy. One or two won't be missed, whoever's they are." Andy said. "I forgot one thing for your list. Stop around that crabby old sign painter's place. You know, old Enscoe. He's got all manner of high quality paint he uses for them billboards in half empty cans. I always used to use it. He'll make you a good deal on some."

I went to work with him shuffling along behind me. I wanted to bring up the Virginia thing, but he was in such a jolly mood I didn't want to bring him down again just then. The wall looked sturdy when I got through with it. It was no glamour job, but serviceable, and I was proud of myself for doing it so simply and cheaply. Andy was all aglow, and to show his gratitude started going through his old wooden boxes that contained fastenings, to find the ones we'd need for the boat project. He got out a box of copper nails and roves (to make rivets) bronze ring nails, bronze bolts, and lags, and woodscrews, and various cleats and chocks and things, and put them on the bench.

35

"We gonna make a sailor outta ya? Or do you have a motor?"

"I was thinking of buying a motor. I have some money saved up from renting out the old schooner and working with Jack. Plus I don't know how to sail."

"Why, ther ain't nothing to it. You just run yer sails up and fiddle and fool 'til you get goin one direction or another. To be a *good* sailor, why, that's a little dif'rent. But every boy should know how. What if you're on a ship that goes down, and you wind up in a lifeboat? They gen'rly have sails in 'em. Or at least they used to. 'Course I don't know how common that is really. But it's good to learn. You got a girlfriend?"

"Yeah, sort of. I guess."

"Best entertainment method to apply to the ladies is to go fer a sail. Your girl like boats?"

"Yeah. But she's better in them than I am. Her old man has a big speed boat he turns her loose in."

"Well, well. You ain't gonna impress her with your little outboard skiff. Does she have a sailboat, too?"

"No, but ... "

"Bingo!"

"But I don't have to impress her. She's pretty cool that way."

"Yeah? She's got the boat. The money. The looks, am I right?"

"Yeah, I guess."

"Then she's in the driver's seat. Son, I've lived many a year, and made many mistakes. Too many to calculate, never mind count. But I've learned a little bit in them years. Now a lot of this is from observation, and some from direct experience. Here's... the most important one when it comes to women: A young feller wants to have all the advantage he can. In later years it's the feller that holds the cards. All except the one concerning 'good sense.' But not for the teenager. It was true when I was a boy, and it's true now, I'll wager.

"You ain't ever gonna save up enough money to outspend her. She's nice, you say, but she ain't exactly falling at your feet. Now, that's fine. But a feller needs confidence, and she's holding most of the cards. I'll tell you how to twist things to your advantage. Does her old man sail?"

"Not that I know of."

"Her mother?"

"No. Nobody, as far as I know."

"Alright. You'll have yer handsome, salty little craft. It'll be purty, and quaint. The girl and her mom will like that. It will be handsome and salty, as I say, and the old man will like that. He won't likely admit it, but I'll tell you it's true.

"Sailing's an art. And you'll already be better at it after your first day than this girl's entire family. They're boaters. They respect somebody who can sail. A fellow

37

running an ocean liner who can't sail scores himself a notch below the ordinary seaman who can. And the girls admire ability. You've got a captive audience. And you'll do clever things in a matter of fact way while she looks on in admiration. It's something you'll never regret knowing. Plus if you get tired of it, you can just clamp an outboard on it anyway. That's what I always done."

Jack and I went out back of Andy's on the "A-Rattle," and spotted a couple of likely cedars near the edge of the cedar swamp. We felled them, and skidded them out one at a time with the tractor.

Jack had brought his flatbed trailer, and we rolled the logs up onto it with a couple of peavys. It was hot damp work, but we had our cedar, and the price was right. The

next day we milled it into one inch flitches at Jack's sawmill, milled up what oak we needed from Jack's stock, and brought all the lumber back to Andy's.

On our way we stopped around the old sign painter's place. Edgar Enscoe was his name. He had a little, cluttered old shop, with miles of ropes and pulleys hanging up that he used for billboards and walls in Atlantic City. He only worked up there occasionally anymore. Mostly he just did little job signs and truck doors. Everything he had—his old truck, his shoes and clothes, his tools, his aluminum scaffold plank, were covered with a zillion splats of color. It all looked kind of psychedelic. But the little gold leaf lettering job he was doing was as neat as a nun's habit, as Jack would say. It was a carved sign; the letters were "incised" with a sharp chisel, and he was gilding and outlining them.

"Pugh," he said without looking up.

"Enscoe," Jack said in response.

"Come to get the truck lettered?"

"I ain't got money enough. Rates a sign painter charges, I could sooner afford a new truck."

"What's the latest name you're using for your mill?"

"Cumberland Sawmill," Jack said. "Has been for years."

"I know you're here for something," Enscoe said. "But let me get off a volley first. I need two white oak two-by-fours, four-foot long, or two and a half by fours, for bumpers. That's what holds the stage up—that is,

39

they go crossways under the stage, at either end, and where they stick out either side they hang in rope stirrups. The ropes and pulleys hook to the stirrups, then to hooks at the top, to go over the top of the billboard or wall you're hanging from. Then there's a wheel put at the end toward the sign, so they don't scratch up your work as you go up. So they gotta be pretty good to do all that. Strong, you know. To hold everything up."

"I get the picture," Jack said. "I guess it's all the time you spend alone that makes you so long winded. I expect we got one on the truck. Boatbuilding lumber. The boy's throwing together a skiff. Good quality stuff. We'll swap you for a coupla gallons of yer fancy paint."

"Hmm," Enscoe said, looking around. "Not a lot extra."

It looked like an awful lot extra to me. He must have read my mind.

"Those are all dedicated to some job or other, you see," he said, looking from can to can.

"Can you undedicate one?" Jack said. "I don't think nobody'd notice."

He shot a look at Jack, then went over and grabbed three different gallon cans—white, beige and grey—that were sitting on a sheet of plywood that had a picture of Eydie Gorme on it.

"She was appearing at the Sands," he said. "She's supposed to come back. But I seem to have misplaced the rest of her. Oh, here's some primer, too. That

40

enough? If not, come back. I'll dig around in the meantime. But it's not a fair swap. The casinos paid for that paint, though I imagine they've written it off by now. How about if I letter your truck?"

Jack twinkled a little. He smiled very rarely. But I knew he secretly admired the official look the lettering gave to my dad's trucks. I hoped he meant some other time, because I was all itchy to get to Andy's and get started. But Enscoe got out a grease pencil and chalk line and walked over to the old truck. He had a little trick where he snapped the chalkline by himself, even as Jack, not realizing it was possible, reached in and tried to snap it for him. Jack, who likes to think of himself as a real expert on things, looked a little sheepish.

He snapped four horizontal lines, then used the string to find the center. From there he scratched out, roughly, in either direction, "Cumberland" on the top, and "Sawmill," just below it, both centered.

Then he struck lines at the bottom and scratched "Delmont, NJ" along the bottom of the door. Then he went and did the same on the other door. Then he got out some goldy-mustardy colored paint and a little quill brush, and about as fast as you could do it with a magic marker, banged out the letters. It was really cool. Then he got a little tub of black paint, washed out the brush, and threw on a little black shadow that made it look three dimensional.

"That old flatbed looks as official as money," Jack said. "Nice color, too."

"Gold always looks good on forest green, or whatever that color is," said Enscoe.

"Now," Jack said, looking at me, "If you decide not to go to college, learn that trade. If you think you got the talent for it. The old lady put me onto the job of lettering the mailbox. 'Robin's Nest,' she wanted, like you would name a plantation or something. I put an entire day into it. Even at my modest rates, it'd be out of the question for anybody to pay me. And that's if it was presentable. Which it sadly ain't, by a long way. Yet Enscoe here could'a done the job in the time it takes a government worker to decide he wants a coffee break. 'Long as nobody chops his fingers off, this man can always make a buck. What's that door lettering worth, Enscoe, when you're not swapping it for a two by four?"

"75 bucks."

"Holy jumpin Jehosephat. And he done it in less than 20 minutes. That's as much as a good lawyer or a mediocre doctor gets for his time. Why ain't you rich as Midas?"

"You saw what I got paid for this one," the painter said.

I decided that if I couldn't learn to paint like that, which I suspected was no easy thing, at least I might get Mr. Enscoe to paint a name on my boat when I finished it.

CHAPTER EIGHT

STARTING THE SKIFF

Jack hung around when we got to Andy's, and asked a million questions and made an equal number of comments. Finally Andy said, "The boy's trynna learn how to make a boat. If you could hold yer questions 'til we're cleaning up, you both might have a chance to learn somethin. Sometimes it's easier to listen with yer mouth closed."

Jack was rather stunned by this, delivered as it was by the tiny, quiet old Andy. But he had such authority when it came to what we were doing that Jack just clammed up, which wasn't his style. I felt bad for him, but I was glad he'd stopped jabbering.

We started by dragging out Andy's "strongback," which was made of two rough-sawn two by tens up on their edges, running parallel about eight inches apart, with two three-foot two-by-eights sticking straight up between them to hold up the molds, as well as ones at each end to hold the stem and transom. The ends also had three foot cross-pieces to hold the contraption upright. Two sawhorse-like stands, only sturdier, joined by three heavy lengthwise planks about 10' long, spaced one and a half feet apart. Then he dug out two "molds," which were frames set up crossways and upright to bend the shape of the boat around. They had notches in the top corners for the "chine logs," that actually run the length of a boat along the bottom, where the side planks and the bottom planks join. They were at the top because we were building the boat upside down.

Then we went into our cedar pile, and got the four best one inch by 17-foot planks we could find. Jack was worried that the cedar was too green, but Andy said that was only a problem for "professional know it alls." Andy had patterns hanging on his wall and using them we made up side planks, cutting and matching boards for both sides. Each side was made up of a top and bottom plank. I had brought along a circular saw, and Andy showed me how to make a cut right down the seam between each pair of planks, using a long plank as a straight edge to run the saw against, so they would fit together perfectly.

Next thing we did was make up a stem out of a 3" by 7" piece of oak, which Andy had patterns for. We cut it out on his table saw, and clamped it to its spot on the strong back. Then we made up a transom from a two by twenty inch by three and a half foot piece of white oak Jack had dug up for the purpose, angling and beveling the sides and the bottom, to specifications Andy seemed to know from memory.

Now it was time to put on the two bottom side planks. We nailed one, then the other, to the stem, so that they went out in a wide vee, after first applying some caulking compound. Then we bent them around the molds until they actually met the transom at the other end. We had to use a "Spanish Windlass," which is a rope wrapped all the way around the planks and joined with a knot, and you put a stick through the ropes in the center and wind them until they draw tight. We drilled and nailed them to the transom, first applying a bedding of caulking again between the planks of the transom. It began to look like a boat. We ripped some one by two oak chines, and after some fiddling, fit them inside the planks at the very bottom, and riveted them to the sides.

How you do that is really cool. You drill a hole the size of the nail you're using and then you drive the copper nail through. Then you drive a copper washer or "rove" over the pointy end that sticks through, and cut the excess off, all but a little bit, with a big wire nipper. Then you hold a sledge hammer against the nail head, and tap the cut off end with a ball peen hammer 'til it starts to flatten out. It took a while to get the hang of it, but once you do, you can keep tapping 'til it starts to draw tight like a nut and bolt.

This might sound boring, but it was one of the funnest things I ever did, so that's why I'm running on about it. Anyway, Andy had me find the center of the transom, and stem, and run a taunt string between the two. He used this to get the boat in line fore and aft and sideways, by measuring every so often, and shifting things around 'til they were exactly centered.

The sides of a boat angle in on the bottom (or out towards the top) so they have to be beveled to take the planking evenly. Andy showed me how to lay a straight edge across the bottom, to see how much it needed to be cut down, then how to use one of his razor sharp block planes to slice lengthwise, never going lower than the inside, or lower edge, so the boat would keep its shape. It took a lot of practice, and by the time we were ready to quit for the day, I was a little discouraged, especially when Andy told me he used to make an entire boat in a day and a half if he was trying, "leisurely two days if I was loafing."

My dad says people's accomplishments always get more impressive the farther they fall into the past and beyond the reach of proof. But seeing how far he got with a rank amateur like me on the first day, I believed him.

Jack, to my complete surprise, said to Andy as we left, "That was good advice, old timer. I learned a lot. So'd the boy."

"Well, you're a fine pair of youngsters," Andy said, "Once a body's got yer attention."

* * *

My head was spinning with all I'd learned, and all the possibilities it seemed to open up to me. But there was no boat building the next day. My dad had a house to raise in Cape May—the owner had gotten tired of every high tide coming into his living room. My Dad needed somebody to drag cribbing to his workers and him as they raised it up.

"The man's in a bit of a hurry, cause he's got renters coming, and any little help me and my elderly crew receive will be most appreciated," he said. So my older sister Kate and I went down with my dad and his two workers, Larson Cole and Roy Thompson. Business was slow, as I've said, so I think my dad wanted to really knock this one out in a hurry to impress the guy, since he owned a lot of property and might have more work, or maybe know others who did. Dad hadn't done a whole lot of work down in Cape May before, so maybe this would open up a new market for him.

I was sorry to see my dad so down about work. He was usually the bigshot, flipping Kate or me a $5 bill if we were going out somewhere. Now he finally had this raising job, and instead of being the bigshot I was used to seeing, he had to hustle like mad to try to prove to the guy that he was worth the money. His two workers, Larson and Roy, were luckily not too hard to please about keeping busy. They came in when he needed them and were fairly content to putter around home when he didn't. The trouble was that they were both over sixty, and couldn't scramble around much any more. Or didn't care to. They had worked for my dad's boss when he was young, and they had been with him now for so long they seemed like family. Anyhow, now my sister and I found ourselves crawling around under this house. Kate is a good sport, but she's a dignified 20-year-old college student, and I knew my dad never intended to have her working like this. That's how I knew he was kind of desperate. He often had me help, but that was different. He never had to depend on me. He always said that you might as well go get a job if you are still breaking your neck in your business and not making ends meet after a lot of years. But of course he was talking about the other guys.

He was still jolly and all, but you could see a little pain in his eyes. We worked hard, and Kate is the type who can make something seem like a fun adventure if she's in the mood, so you could say we made the best of it.

"How's Lisa doing these days?" Kate asked as we were relaxing after dinner.

How indeed, I thought. Lisa's my girlfriend, sort of. When I work with Jack, up at his sawmill in Cumberland County, I see her quite a bit because she lives up that way. Not much was shaking these days at the mill, so we had dropped off a little. She works at a little greasy diner Jack calls "Flatfoot's," after its injured owner, and her parents have a big boat yard and two oyster boats up on the Maurice River. In a way she's big time compared to me, but she doesn't see it that way, because people from her neck of the woods are considered by some to be, well, hicks. It's kind of complicated. Anyway, neither of us drive, so its a hassle to get together if I'm not working up there. And if I don't see her, I worry about what she's doing, and who she's seeing, so the whole thing gets to be a chore after a while, so I sometimes put it out of my head. That's Leon's advice. He says it will "preserve my sanity." But now it was back in my head, so I gave her a call.

She was glad to hear from me, and I ran on about the boat Andy and I were building, and then we got on to the Virginia story. That got her attention. She loves a good mystery. So I promised I'd get more details, and we'd get together and puzzle it out.

* * *

The next day my dad didn't need me so I went on down to Andy's. We fiddled around with some bottom planking, and the boat started really looking like something. It took some time to bevel the edges and fit them right—longer than I expected. I'm afraid I wasn't too patient. I wanted to work all night, I was so excited with the progress, but I could see Andy was running out of gas, so we quit about five o'clock. We sat around and talked a while, admiring our work.

The talk tapered off, after a bit, and we sat in silence a little while. Then Andy said, "All this cedar sawing puts me in mind of my girl. She set around the shop many a time and watched and chatted with me while I worked. She didn't have a lot of friends. They thought she was a little odd. Chatter, chatter. I didn't follow a lot of it. She was crazy about birds, though. All sorts of wildlife. She'd tell me all about the things she saw. She'd draw pictures, and write in her little journal. It wasn't what other girls her age was doing. Ther's stacks of that stuff in her bedroom. When she got older, I made her that boat you seen, and she sailed all over these back waters, writin', and sketchin'. She took me out to see eagle's nests one time. They was thriving one year, empty the next. DDT, she said. Sprayed by the Mosquito Commission. I didn't rightly believe her then, though I didn't tell her so. But now I see that's exactly the fact. She was ahead of her time. That boat of hers was called the 'Rachel,' after a woman by the name of

Rachel Carson who Virginia thought the world of. This Rachel wrote a book about DDT and all the other poisons, and how bad they was. It caused a lot of trouble. Virginia wrote back and forth with her. She went on down to the Mosquito Commission and told them, nice and friendly, how them poisons was a big mistake. I used to drive her down. But I didn't go inside. I sat in my pickup 'til she was done.

"Well, Lordy. You'd 'a thought she said all their mom's was communists the way they took on. Why, they called her a communist. And a fruit cake. Said all of science was on their side. No one but a coupla 'hysterical women kooks' agreed with her. Virginia was real disappointed. She was only trying to help. She'd set and cry out here, to think about all the harm she thought that stuff was doing. She wasn't much into carpentry and all, like I was. She was very different from me. But I'll tell you something. One day your old friend Jack Pugh was around here, and Virginia was in the corner poring over one of her books. Jack says to me something like this:

"Jackson, the world ain't fair. You and me works with our hands, a-butcherin wood, and could use a little help. Now I got stuck with nothin but useless girls, and you got that pretty miss there with her head in the clouds, not doing you a bit of good. Coupla husky sons is what we should'a' been dealt, by rights.

"'Pugh,' I says to him. I remember it clear as if it was yesterday. 'Pugh,' I says, 'I could'a been given a son, and he mighta been no damn good. But God gave me Virginia. And she's an angel.'"

"'Yer a sap, Jackson,' Pugh said to me. 'Ain't none of them angels.'"

"I didn't take too kindly to him saying that in front of my girl like that, and I didn't show him much courtesy for many years. But he ain't nearly so full of himself as he once was."

I didn't know what to say. So I said nothing for a while. Then I said, "Sorry she died, Andy. She was so young and all."

"Too young, son. And thanks."

We sat a while longer. Then I got my courage up to ask about how it happened. "So what happened?," I asked, "Did she just fall overboard?"

Andy looked at me, and for a minute I regretted asking the question.

"Virginia didn't just fall overboard," he finally said. "It wasn't no accident. There ain't no use stirring people up after all these years, so I won't burden your young head with the details. But there's a soul that can't rest easy, and some folks that don't deserve too, on account of that incident."

I wanted to say, "Burden me, my girlfriend and I want to know." But I felt like I'd gone far enough into his personal stuff for one day.

CHAPTER NINE

THE JOURNAL

So, I thought. That's why Jack is a little cool to Andy, and yet wanted me to help him out. I got on the horn with Lisa that night, and we decided to get together and puzzle on it a little. She said her dad had to run down to Cape May to pick up some sheaves for one of his oysterboats, so he'd drop her off if I could arrange to run her back, which I figured I could since I'd worked up a few brownie points helping my dad.

She was interested in the boat we were building, and she hadn't seen my Depression tractor, so when she arrived we combined the two: I drove her over to Andy's on the ancient machine.

The tractor impressed her, in a way, but I could tell she thought it was a little Beverly Hillbillyish. I thought she'd be spooked by Andy and his little shack, but she didn't seem to be. She was more concerned with getting the circulation back into her "bee-hind" from the hard tractor seat.

Andy was delighted, to put it mildly, with his new guest. His eyes lit up to their maximum level, and he tried to make excuses for the place's humble appearance while I made the introductions.

"We ain't had such beauty in this old chicken coop since, well, for a long time, let's say that."

"Joe's been telling me all about you, Mr. Jackson," Lisa said. "My family has a boat yard, and I've always loved boats. I guess I didn't really have much choice. Do you think I could see the one you two fellas are building?"

Andy shuffled off ahead of us at his modest pace, trying to neaten up as he went. It was a dark, cramped little place, with a kind of funny smell, but when you got in the shop part it was brighter, and the freshly cut cedar improved the odor problem.

Boats really look cool "a-building," as Andy called it. At least all the pictures I'd seen, and certainly this one, did. I was proud to see that Lisa was impressed. The boat looked big and important there in the shed. It made me really want to finish it, and in a way, I was sorry not to be working on it today. But I wasn't sorry I'd brought Lisa over to see it, so it was okay.

"Seeing your youth and feminine beauty puts me in mind of my late daughter. She wasn't as sparkly as you, but was, like you, quite lovely. She was sweet, what I mean. But she was so cussed shy around people is all. She could handle a skiff, though. And she seemed content to spend endless hours by herself out on the water, or in the woods, with just her sketch pad and notebook."

"She drew pictures?" Lisa asked. "I like to do watercolors."

"So did she, sweetheart. Would you like to see some?"

Man, that Lisa was sure an ice breaker. I had wanted to get a look at her stuff, but it seemed too personal a thing to ask. At least just yet. We followed the old man as he slowly made his way to a little back room up in the house part of the building. I was startled when he opened the door, because it was so clean and colorful compared to the rest of the house. It was almost wall-papered with pictures of birds and plants and wildlife. There was a desk and a bookshelf crammed with books, and a pretty bed, all of which Andy had made for her, and a bureau and what Andy called a "flat file," all crammed into the room. But it looked tidy.

"She wouldn't never hang up her own pictures," Andy said. "Too shy to. Even in her own room. Them's all prints and other people's work. Her stuff's in here." He opened the top drawer of the flat file and gently lifted out a watercolor of some wildflowers. It was extremely neat and beautiful. Lisa and I both gasped.

"Now I don't hang 'em up because they might get ruined. Which is rather stupid, because nobody sees 'em." He pulled out some more, different kinds of plants and flowers, then some birds and small animals. Another drawer had pen and ink sketches. Still another had pencil sketches; some of people, some of trees, some of animals.

He went all the way to the bottom drawer and pulled out a picture of a bird laying on the ground. It was some kind of an egret or heron.

"These is the ones she was working on right at the end. They're the birds and things she found dead after

Rudy Smick would spray the meadow. Here's a dragonfly. Ain't it beautiful? She said they floated down the creeks and sluices by the hundreds after he'd gone over with his DDT. Now, myself, I wasn't one to go all mushy over dead bugs, but I got an idea everything's got its place in the world. That's what Virginia told me then, and I know she was right."

"These should be in a gallery somewhere," Lisa said. "They're beautiful. I wish I could paint or draw one-tenth as well as that."

Andy began putting them all carefully back, and we watched in silence. When he was done, I said, "She used to write stuff, too, didn't she?"

Andy fixed me with a look, like I'd gone over the line.

"I'd love to read some of her stuff sometime." Lisa put in. "I bet it's great, judging by her artwork." For some reason Andy was less put off by Lisa than me. He suddenly looked less stricken. "I bet in her heart she hoped somebody would read her writing, and see her artwork." Lisa went on. "I'm embarrassed by my stuff, but at the same time I wish people could see it, you know what I mean? And yet Joe hasn't even seen any of it."

"I 'spect you're right, little girl. I 'spect Virginia would, too, if it's the right people." He went over to her desk, opened a drawer, pulled out a thick, bound composition book, and handed it to Lisa. "Now you look after that," he said.

***

I was a little put out that he handed it over to Lisa so easy, after he'd only just met her. Lisa could tell, and later she said I shouldn't let it bother me. She said it was something about her being a girl and reminding him of Virginia. She said Andy probably figured a girl would understand Virginia better. "He wouldn't think of showing me how to build a boat," she said by way of explanation.

My sister Kate drove us over to the Avalon boardwalk in her old Volvo, then later on picked us up after visiting one of her friends over there, and drove us all the way to Dorchester to drop Lisa off. She's an awful good sister that way. On the way home I told her a little bit about Virginia, and about how Lisa came to get the journal, which she took home with her, and some other stuff. And Kate settled my mind about it like she often does. She said Andy was my friend, but he couldn't talk to me the same way he could Lisa, especially about Virginia. He communicated with me in a different way. And Lisa wasn't really taking over. It showed she was serious about me to want to get involved in the whole Andy-Virginia caper. I wasn't so sure, but Kate was usually right. She would give me bad news just as quick, if she thought I needed to hear it.

"Oh, by the way, sailor boy," she said after we'd hashed out the Lisa thing, "My friend Cindy," who she'd been to see that night, "does a lot of sailing. She sailed Sunfish, then Comets, over at the yacht club for years.

56

Said she'd be glad to take you out to give you some sailing pointers."

Andy and I worked most of the next day finishing up the bottom planking, and when we were done, she really looked like a boat.

On one edge of each plank Andy had me plane a slight bevel before we nailed it on, so the boards wouldn't buckle when they swelled with water. Then he'd showed me how to drive caulking cotton into the seams deep enough to cut into each edge to dig in when the boards swelled, so that there would be no gaps for water to come through. Where the boards were nailed to the chines and side-planks at each end (they go crossways on the boat) a generous bead of goopy caulk gets laid down so that it squeezes out of the seam as the plank is drawn fast. When we were finally done it looked watertight to me.

The last thing we did for the day was to flip the boat upright, which was easy with the overhead falls that hung from the rafters, and pop the molds out.

The boat looked almost ready to put in the water, and my heart beat fast to see it, but Andy said we were less than halfway done, which I found hard to believe.

* * *

"There are a couple of names," Lisa said, "that keep coming up in this journal. Besides Rachel Carson, I mean. One of them is Weston MacBride. At first she calls him Weston MacBride. Then later it's Weston, and towards the end, Westy. He seems to be a sculptor, and

57

also to have a great interest in birds. And if I'm not mistaken, Virginia had a great interest in him."

"Oh yeah?" I said. "Who's the other one?"

"T. Everett Tyree. Or T.E. Tyree, as it says on the side of his truck, according to Virginia. 'Westy' calls him 'Tee-Hee' Tyree. Tee Hee is not fond of Virginia or Westy, from what I can tell. He had a big farm in Goshen and was friendly with the Mosquito Commission. She claims they dug him a duck pond (in the name of mosquito control) where he brings 'dudes' to hunt. She and MacBride liked to go back there to look at birds and things, and apparently MacBride got into big confrontations with T.E. and his hunting parties because they would shoot the migrating hawks. Also, apparently, the Cape May County Mosquito Commission sprayed DDT on TeeHee's crops, which saved him spraying them. There are a couple of letters from Rachel Carson, that seem to respond to ones to her from Virginia, and the two of them seem pretty sure that DDT is really terrible for everybody, and makes for more insect pests as well. I'm not sure why. I looked in the phone book up here, but I didn't see any Weston or W. McBride. Anyway, he's most likely from down your way. I bet if we found him, he would have some good information."

After we hung, up I got out the phone book, and after finding nothing likely under "McBride," I got the bright idea to look up "MacBride." There was only one. "MacBride, Weston P. Mechanic and Main Street, CMCH," and the number. My heart beat fast. I sat for a minute looking at the page. I felt excited, but then

58

uneasy. I thought about calling, then lost heart. The phone, which was sitting right next to me, suddenly rang. I jumped, then picked it up.

"Hello . . . ?"

"Did you find it?"

"Yeah, right here. I was just going to call."

"Great. Good luck. Bye."

Now I was stuck. I dialed the number. It rang once, twice, three times.

I began to feel relief after the fifth ring, then it was picked up. "Ha-llo," said a scratchy, annoyed voice."

"Hello. Uh. Mr. West, er, MacBride?"

"Yes."

"This is Joe Bass. From South Dennis."

"Yes."

"I wanted to, uh, ask you. Well talk, um."

"Go ahead." He was losing patience.

"Did you ever know a girl named Virginia Jackson?"

Silence.

Then, after a bit:

"*Who* is this?"

"Joe Bass."

"And why, Joe Bass, do you want to know?"

"Well, I know her father, and he kind of is interested. Well, I'm not sure what happened to Virginia. I mean, I know she died. But Andy's not quite sure how it happened. But it was some kind of foul play, he thinks."

"But why do *you* want to know?" I was stuck on that one. "Who are you, anyway?"

"Andy said, 'there is a soul that can't rest easy,'" I said, that sounded good. "Virginia, I guess he means. 'And some that don't deserve to,' which makes me think somebody got away with something they shouldn't have. I'd like to ease the old man's mind a little if I could."

"I'm not so sure opening this can of worms will ease anyone's mind. How old are you, anyhow?"

"Fifteen."

"Hmm. Write down your questions. Young people can still write, can't they? I'll give you my address. Mail them to me, and I'll answer as I see fit. Goodbye."

He didn't give me his address, but of course it was right there in the phone book. I called Lisa and told her about it. She said the guy sounded really intriguing, and that we should each scratch out some questions.

CHAPTER TEN

THE SAILING LESSON

"Joe—undo the main sheet, there, and take out the boom crutch."

"Hold on, there Cindy," I said. "What's the mainsheet?"

"Oh, yeah. You don't know much about it. Sorry. This is the main sheet. There's the main halyard. This is the jib sheet and the jib halyard . . ."

My head began to cloud up. Kate's friend Cindy was taking me out in her Comet sailboat to teach me how to sail, and she was wearing a top that was just a little bit less than equal to its task, and those kind of baggy boxer shorts girls wear, which were riding low and showing the top of a really brief, from what I could tell, thong-like bikini bottom. So already I was at a disadvantage. She was Kate's age, and very attractive, but not, as far as I could tell, aware that I was anymore than a little kid in need of some sailing instruction, which I was, of course, but I was getting so distracted by her I was afraid I was going to really goof up big time.

I kept pulling the wrong rope, or "sheet," and getting in the way of the boom or tiller or God knows what. It was a 16-foot boat with a fairly cramped cockpit that had a big centerboard trunk in the middle, and Cindy practically had to climb over me sometimes to straighten things out. You can imagine how this affected my concentration.

Finally we got into a big sound, which is like a lake out in the marshes, where we could just sail along in one direction for a while, instead of tacking and reaching and running up the waterway, between boats and buoys and such.

"Take the tiller," she said, as we squeezed past each other. "Turn a little in each direction, and ease in and out on the sheet, and you'll get a feel for how things work. Steer generally for that Osprey nest on the other side. I might as well get a little sun while I'm out here."

Off came the baggy shorts, which she stuck up under the foredeck, requiring her to get down on her knees and elbows with her basically uncovered posterior pointing up at me. We were both on the right, or starboard side, and the boat was "heeling," or leaning the other way.

Wham! The boom flipped around and smacked the stays, (the wires that hold the mast up), grazing the top of my head on its way, and tilting the boat away over to the side we were both on—formerly the high side—and the next thing I knew we were both in the water and the boat was laying on its side and filling with water.

"Nice going, Popeye," Cindy gasped and gurgled as we floundered in the bay. "Come on, quick, before she fills up any more."

She motioned me to follow her around to the other side of the boat, where we stood on the centerboard and rocked it upright, with some effort.

"I thought I told you about jibing," she said as we bailed out the boat with a plastic scoop and one of my shoes. *You probably did,* I thought. "Weren't you looking where you were going? Man."

I was thoroughly embarrassed, to the point where I could feel the skin burning on my face. Or was that the sun?

"I'm sorry," she said, after we'd gotten things righted up again. "I thought you'd catch on a little faster."

Oh, thanks, I thought.

But the dunking actually did me some good. I was mortified, but on the other hand it could hardly get worse. Cindy wasn't any less distracting now that she was all wet, but I was concentrating a little better all the same. We actually began to chuckle about our "knockdown" after a bit, and Cindy cheered up and got kind of chatty. She said something similar had happened to her when her older sister Stephanie first tried to teach her to fly an airplane.

"You can fly an airplane?" I asked.

"Not very well. Stephanie can fly anything. Taildraggers, Twins. She took me up in a Piper Warrior one time, which is supposed to be very easy to fly. I thought it would be a cinch. But she kept drilling me with instructions about the controls, the instruments, stalls, engine outs until my head was spinning. When she handed over the controls, I was scared to death that when I banked to turn the plane would keep right on going and flip over, or nose dive. I was tight as a drum. And when I tried to take it in for a landing, I was wagging around so bad, because a plane is hard to control at low speeds, that even Steph looked a little concerned. I tried to set the plane down like she told me, but we started arguing, and I stalled the plane too high off the ground. The tail hit first with a big bang, then we pitched forward and Stephanie took over the controls and pulled us out of it. It was pretty wild. Those planes are small, and you feel pretty vulnerable banging around in them."

"Now I don't feel so bad. Did you ever get any more flying lessons?"

"Once in a while, but she hasn't let me land yet. She flies banner planes, and she took me up in one of them one time—a Super Cub, where you sit fore and aft, and fly with a stick, instead of a yoke. That's pretty cool. Have you ever been flying?"

"Yeah," I said proudly. "I've been up a couple of times in Jack Pugh's Stearman."

"Oh, yeah, I remember that. You were in the paper over that murder case, and they talked about you guys landing on the beach and all. Steph would love to check out that old plane. She flies an old retired cropduster for the banner company—a Piper Pawnee, I think—but she'd really love to get her hands on an old bi-plane."

We chatted along, me saying I'd be glad to hook up her sister and old Jack—or that she could call him directly; her saying I was learning quite well, and she was sure her sister would pursue the Stearman angle. By the time we got back to her dock, I had a decent handle on reaching, running, beating, etc., which are all ways you sail depending on your intended direction and the direction of the wind. And I even learned a little about flying. I figured I could sail a boat if I had to. And I could hardly close my eyes for sometime afterward without seeing Cindy from one of the many interesting angles I'd seen her from that day. As a result, all those sailing words have kind of a nice, warm ring to them, since I can't think of them separately from the shapely person who taught them to me. At the time it was almost more distracting than it was enjoyable. Nah. On second thought I guess it wasn't. Anyhow, "sailing" and

"Cindy" have always gone together in my mind since that day. I wonder if "Joe" and "overturned sailboat" go together in hers, or if she ever thought about her role in that little disaster.

When I told Lisa that I had been "brushing up on my sailing" with one of Kate's friends, I didn't emphasize the fleshy part, but she was mighty interested in my "instructor" all the same.

CHAPTER ELEVEN

SPARS AND A CENTERBOARD

Andy seemed glad to see me, and we got right to work putting the ribs in, then the sheer clamp and an inwale, which is a thin board up along the gunnel inside the ribs that helps stiffen the boat and acts as a hand-hold. We nailed and screwed and riveted them all together, and sawed off the ribs with a hand saw where they stuck up past the sheerline.

"She'd be right near done, if you was making a row boat or power skiff. But we gotta undertake to install a centerboard," Andy said.

We laid in a keelson out of one inch cedar, which is a board that runs down the center of the bottom, on the inside, for the length of the boat. We tilted the boat up on its side and riveted it to the bottom boards. Then about one third of the way back from the stem, Andy marked out a slot to be cut with a Skilsaw. I cut it as neatly as I could, and Andy slowly chiseled out the ends square. Then he marked out two pieces of plywood for me to cut out in a rectangle, then two pieces of oak, one and a half inches times the width of the slot, for each end. But before we fastened them, we cut two more oak strips the length of the plywood trunk boards, and gooped them up and screwed them to one edge of each of the trunk beds. We turned them to the outside on the bottom, then gooped and fastened the first two oak pieces vertically between the trunk boards at each end, sticking out the bottom the same distance of the thickness of the bottom, keelson included. It sounds complicated, but when you see it it makes sense.

Next we gooped up the ends that stuck out and the bottoms of the side strips, and jammed the ends down into the slot, and fastened the long pieces down to the keelson with screws. Oh, yeah. We also fastened strips along the tip (from what would become the inside) just like we had on the bottom, but if I had told you then it would be confusing. Plus I forgot. Anyhow, Andy made up a thwart, or seat, which fastened to the forward end of the trunk in the center, then to a "seat clamp," or lengthwise strip that ran along the ribs on either side. This gives you a place to sit and keeps the trunk from wobbling.

That was enough for one day. The next day I spent a while getting the bushing and pin out of Virginia's old centerboard trunk, was well as her old centerboard, which we used for a pattern to make our centerboard. It was five eighths inch thick, and our plywood was one half inch, so Andy hoped ours would be stout enough. We drilled through the trunk, set the pin in the right spot, and lined up the centerboard.

Andy screwed a piece of bronze halfoval rubbing strip along the bottom edge of the board, so it would have a tendency to sink, and then screwed on the nifty bronze handle that had been on Virginia's centerboard to pull it up and down. There, in the shop, we had a good, working model.

"Let's find us some spars," Andy said when we were done, and we both climbed onto the A-rattle and putted out behind his house down the narrow overgrown road that led to the cedar swamp.

* * *

We had brought along one of Andy's sharp handsaws and a razor-edged hatchet, so it took less time to fell and limb our victims than it did for Andy to select them, which took a lot of chin scratching and "humph'ing."

I had no real idea how the boat was going to be rigged, but Andy had me cut our stoutest sapling to about 12 feet long, then directed me in skinning and shaping it, first with a drawknife, then with a little, curved spokeshave.

It took forever, and Andy never was completely satisfied, but finally he let me attack the other two, which were thinner. I trimmed them down to about one and three quarter inches, compared to the two and a half inches of the heavier one, and he was quite as particular about these. I was a little better at handling the tools by now, so it went a lot more smoothly, to a point where it actually got to be kind of enjoyable.

CHAPTER TWELVE

WESTON AND VIRGINIA

That night Lisa and I got together over the phone to try and put together our questions for Weston MacBride

We didn't know how to approach it exactly. Everything we thought of either sounded stupid or like it might put this MacBride guy off. Then we decided to outline our problem on paper, so we hung up so we could each come up with our own version. When I called back, we found out we were pretty close, and from our outline we came up with what we thought were decent questions.

Here's what we came up with:

1. How well did you know Miss Jackson?

2. Where were you when the mishap (her death) occurred?

3. Did the police question you? If so, what information did you give them?

4. Do you have any reason to suspect foul play? Can you point to any individual you're suspicious of?

5. Can you give us any other information that might help us clear up this matter?

To make them look official, I figured they should be typed, and since I didn't dare use my dad's typewriter, I shot over to Freddy's on my bike. But he wasn't there. So I took a chance and rode over to Leon's. His Pop seemed glad to see me, as if the conversation about

Virginia Jackson was forgotten. He let me in, and when Leon and I got off by ourselves, I slipped him the list of questions. He read through them with a sort of critical look on his face, but didn't suggest any changes, which wasn't like him.

"We're going up to your office to use your typewriter for a report Joe's doing, Pop."

"Anything for Joe's education," Pop said cheerfully.

I filled Leon in as best I could about Lisa's and my ideas about Weston and all, and Leon banged the questions out—in fact he made two copies—in short order.

The next day I sealed the questions in an envelope and sent them off with my return address. Lisa and I had been going through Virginia's diaries—mostly she was reading bits and pieces over the telephone to me, which started to get on my nerves. But then she got the bright idea to run off copies of some of the stuff over at the Township Hall, which was right down the road from her house. We worried that it might not exactly be the best idea from a legal point of view, but we allowed that since we were doing an investigation, which was for Andy's, and in a way, Virginia's benefit, it was probably okay, especially if we didn't tell anyone. She sent me the copies and I sent her a copy of the questions. It seemed silly to mail things such a short distance, but it actually is pretty quick.

* * *

Virginia was real heartbroken about the birds and things. She wrote down things Rachel Carson told her, and had some letters Rachel Carson had sent her stapled into the diary in a couple of places. Rachel Carson had discovered that DDT did all kinds of harm to animals' reproductive cycles, and that bugs, since they're more primitive, could develop resistance, which didn't happen to their predators, which were higher on the chain, so you wound up with more bugs. There was a lot of stuff like that, and even more complicated, so we kind of skimmed through it.

What wasn't complicated was how people treated her who disagreed with what she said. Even real smart people like scientists made stupid responses to her, some of which she wrote down in her journal, like "it's too hard for a young girl like you to understand," or "you're too emotional." "Your sex is not given to reason," was another. Lisa went into orbit over that. And people at the Mosquito Commission said she was a communist, and an agitator, and they also said "emotional female" and that kind of stuff.

Maybe I was prejudiced because I was looking at it through her words, but the other side sure wasn't very convincing. Then there was a bit about a visit her father had gotten from Rudy Smick and Clarence Berman (that's Leon's "Pop,") telling him that she should lay off, that there was a lot of money at stake. Rudy offered to buy some of her paintings, which was to try and shut her up,

Virginia found out, because she sold him two, not realizing, and she later heard that they were throwing darts at them and having a big laugh at the Mosquito Commission.

At first her father only mentioned that Rudy and Clarence had come around, and didn't tell her what and all they said. So when Rudy came around later, and said stuff like, "now you're being a sensible girl," and offering to set her up with his son, and kind of eyeing her up like he wanted to go out with her, old as he was (this is all told in the diary), she didn't know what to make of his sudden change of attitude, or the bit about being "sensible," though she did say she found him "disgusting."

But when she quizzed Andy, he told her about what they had said, and she got real mad at him, which must have been rare because it really shook her up, and that's when she started meeting up with Weston MacBride more and writing what he had to say, which was often quite a lot.

They had first met out behind Hand's meadow on Sluice Creek. He was walking the dike with his binoculars, and she sailed by in her skiff.

He pointed out an eagle, which she hadn't seen. Then she invited him to ride out to Mosquito Point in the skiff to see the short-eared owls. She wrote that she was a "little too daring, inviting a strange man into my boat," but he seemed so mesmerized by the bird, and the meadows, and spoke so "eloquently," as she put it, that she thought he must be a "kindred spirit, and could never be a violent man with such a poetic heart." Later in the journal, after going on about Mr. MacBride, she came back to that idea, and said "God, I hope I'm right. We plan to meet again."

From what I could tell, this Weston talked her ears nearly flat. "Mr. MacBride spoke at great length about" such and such, she was always saying. She wrote like somebody in an old time novel, like Anne of Green Gables or something, especially when she'd been talking to "Mr. MacBride." She sure must have stuck out in South Dennis if she actually spoke that way.

This Weston got her more fired up than ever, and she started writing letters to the paper and to the Mosquito Commission. He didn't seem to go to the meetings himself, but gave Virginia all kinds of ideas of what to say, as if she needed them.

CHAPTER THIRTEEN

THE INTERVIEW

I was heading out the door to go to Andy's when my mother handed me a letter, with a curious look in her eye; it had Weston MacBride's name and return address printed on the envelope. I didn't expect a response so soon, so it took a second to register what it might be.

When I opened it, after trying to act nonchalant about it to my mother, I was kind of surprised to see what he had to say. I had expected answers to our questions. Numbered, even. But here's what he said:

Dear Mr. Bass,

Your questions seem to be beneath your apparent inquisitive intellect. Too much Hardy boys, or perhaps, that dreaded invention, television.

The questions would be offensive if taken at face value, but I'm willing to give you a chance to redeem yourself. To do so I would request that you answer a couple of my questions. To wit:

1. Have you read Silent Spring? If not, do so. If so, what is your perception of the effects of pesticides on the environment?

2. *What do you know of Mosquito Commission practices? This matter will lack context if you don't acquaint yourself with these things.*

3. *Similarly, how familiar are you with our county governing body? Make it your business to understand them fully if you do not already.*

4. *Please let me know how Andrew Jackson is getting along, and whether he has preserved Miss Jackson's artwork, which is (was) so exquisite.*

If you are interested in following up this matter, I am anxious to help, provided your sincerity is adequately demonstrated.

Very truly yours,

Weston MacBride

I didn't know what to make of that letter. I put it in my pocket and walked outside to my Depression tractor. I had changed my mind about going to Andy's. I figured I'd fire the old girl up and just cruise around a little, maybe over to Freddy's, before it got dark. I wasn't too anxious to show the letter to Lisa, or read it to her, because it made our questions, and us, look foolish.

But the stupid tractor wouldn't start: I ran down the battery trying to get it going. Then I cranked it until my arm was numb. I could have looked up my father, but

I'm pretty sure he would have told me to try and solve it myself. So I tried. I messed with the carburetor. It was getting gas. I checked the fire, which was hard to do, because by now I had to crank it by hand. I wound up holding a plug wire and giving myself a shock, which isn't real pleasant, because I couldn't reach the coil and crank the engine over at the same time. I knew my dad or Jack or Freddy's dad would just poke or fiddle, and she'd go right off. But not me. It was almost like my lack of confidence did me in. Like the motor was mocking me. It happened with lawnmowers, outboards, everything. My dad would come up, with a look like "you'll start, you S.O.B., or else," and the engine would knuckle right under.

Fire, air, compression, fuel. I had all of those. So I gritted my teeth, growled at the old engine, and gave the crank a mighty heave.

"Fire?"

It was Jack, the "A-Rattle King," who claimed to be able to "sense the presence of sick A-Rattles and go to them." He had walked right up on me.

"Air?"

"Yeah, Yeah. Compression. Fuel."

"Like I told you."

"Yeah. You and everybody else."

"She oughtta start."

"I know."

"Somethin' stinks. Wha-I-mean, we got a nimrod for a mechanic. Or a nitwit. Or a nincompoop. Whatever."

"Thank's Jack."

"Key on?"

"Key's on."

Jack popped off the distributor cap, and peered inside it with his fiercest squint. He got out his little worn down pen-knife and scraped and poked. He got out his handkerchief and wiped the inside of it. He popped off the rotor, pulled out the points, scraped them. He put it all back together. Still looking at the distributor, he pointed toward the crank.

"Start her up." he said.

"Yeah, right," I thought. I gave it a half hearted crank. She fired once. Jack, still looking at the engine, made a circular motion with his finger, like "crank some more." I gave it a swing.

"Put-put-pt.pt.pt. ..." she was off. Just like that.

"Little cold-blooded," Jack said. "Points was c'roded. Cap a little damp. Just needed a tickle."

This didn't help my mechanical confidence.

"Anybody can rebuild an engine, or put on brakes, or that type thing. Takes a sixth sense to know how to tickle a bad-humored engine 'til you get a smile out of her. Touch her in the wrong spot, and you get slapped. Then you need a court order and an act of Congress to get her started. Anything new with your boat-building buddy and his dead daughter?"

I told him a little about the diaries and stuff. I figured if he could understand motors that way, he was no doubt more likely than me to see something in this whole Virginia mystery, so I described what Lisa and I had been up to and what we had learned since Jack and I had talked about the subject, told him about our questions, and handed him the response from Weston MacBride.

He read it with a lot of grimaces and eyebrow raising. When he was done he said:

"This Weston character is a twit, far as I can tell. A grown man oughtn't put on such airs. Needs a smart rap on the side of the head. Trying to make you pups look stupid. Very brave to make fun of kids. Let's go see him. We got his address."

What the heck, I thought. I wasn't feeling real confident about talking to this guy on my own, or writing to him, or whatever. I could tell Lisa about it later. I went in and told my mother that Jack and I were going to run out to Jamesway in Cape May Court House to get some oil and stuff for the tractor. All she said is "Are you sure you want to ride with him?"

I wasn't, really, but it had been so long since our last ride that I threw caution to the wind.

* * * *

Cape May Court House isn't that far from my house—seven miles or so—but I forgot how much longer

79

trips were with Jack at the helm. We putted along with the usual backlog of impatient tailgaters, Jack cursing and fuming at them, peering at the rearview mirror saying "we're developing a tail. Damn." It was hard to plan for our conversation with MacBride, since Jack was so preoccupied with the cars behind him and blathering instead of speeding up past 30 miles per hour.

When we got to Mechanic Street, I had to keep repeating the address as Jack inched along, until we finally came to a nice, stately looking house with the right number on the door.

Weston MacBride was a lot older than I'd expected. Of course I knew it had been a long time ago, but Virginia's diary described a "noble, striking man," "tall and robust," and a lot younger. He *was* tall. And he had a kind of fierce dark eyed look, with a furrow in the middle of his forehead like he was always a little curious and a little angry. He had unkempt grey hair and bushy grey eyebrows.

"Joe Bass, Jr.," I said. "And this is my friend Jack Pugh."

"Weston MacBride. Come in." He didn't seem surprised at all that I had come, or that Jack was with me. I was surprised, though, by the inside of his house. It was chock full of sculptures—clay, stone, bronze. He had a big wire skeleton like thing in the middle of the living room with clay glopped on it like he was molding up a statute. He had shelves of little heads and carved animals and things I couldn't recognize. He had a big piece of marble with fish and things carved into the front of it. There were some things carved out of wood—not decoys, but odd sort of stuff. There were also paintings and prints on the walls, mostly with a lot of dust on them.

"I guess these things is hard to unload. You've built up quite an inventory." Jack said after squinting around with his mouth open.

Mr. MacBride didn't say anything. He just motioned us in to another room, pointed to a two-foot high sculpture of a naked woman on a little heavy duty stand in a corner of the room.

"Virginia," he said, gesturing his hand at it.

"Land of Goshen," Jack said, looking all around it. "Not a stitch. A hell of a lot better scantlings than her old man."

"Well, she was special," Mr. MacBride said.

I felt pretty weird. I had thought of her as this straight laced, innocent girl, and had kind of pictured her looks like you do when you don't really know what they look like. This wasn't what I'd imagined. MacBride rubbed his hand on her shoulders, like she was alive. And she looked pretty shiny all over—some places more than others.

"A bronze casting. Very costly," he said.

"You got any more? What I mean, you cast more than one, didn't you?"

"Are you a collector?"

81

"My Bert is somethin' of an Art Lover."

But that's all MacBride said about it.

"Come. Sit down. I'll get us coffee." We went into his dingy little kitchen. It had bare spots in the linoleum floor, where very worn wood showed through. Around the edges of the bare spots were hundreds of little tacks holding the linoleum lip down. He had the most mish-mashed set of cups and plates and little burnt pans you ever saw. They were all clean, though and stacked up on a little jelly cupboard thing.

He put water in a tiny, burnt-looking sauce pan and fired up the gas burner, set up a little percolator with coffee for when it boiled, and sat down.

It was strange in that house. Even Jack couldn't find much to say.

"As I'm sure you've been able to ascertain, Virginia was, is, very important to me," Weston said. "I don't suffer fools or triflers gladly. You two have the look of sincerity, if not great sagacity, and I admire things genuine, however modest. You, young Bass, seem ready to persevere and are no doubt filled with the optimism of the young. No doubt your septaugenarian friend is filled with the wisdom of years of relatively fruitless struggle..."

"And you're full of yourself. You're, what-I-mean, a twit, as I told the boy when he showed me the letter you sent him. The boy turned to you 'cause he feels bad for a little old man name O'Jackson that ain't got

82

no joy outta life since he lost his daughter. I got a hole in his chest, as you may say, and the boy aims to plug it up just a little by getting back some of that girl's credit when she died in an unexplained way and some shifty people that tried to pass her off as a kook avoided the scrutiny of the authorities. I ain't saying I know who done it. I'm sayin' there's people whose hands is dirty and won't let this girl rest in peace as long as her pop, a man more ancient and shriveled and pitiful than myself, wanders around dazed, with a broken heart and a troubled mind. The boy may be stirring up a can of worms that makes people uncomfortable, but this girl had a pure heart from what I can tell, and she was treated accordingly. That is to say disgraceful, as gen'ly happens to the good ones. Something stinks, what I mean. Everybody knew it then. The boy knows it now. I expect you can help us if you want to, but if you're just going to make fun of us and show off your big words, we got better things to do. You ain't the normalest man in the world yourself, you know. But luckily I ain't the sarcastic type. What's it gonna be?"

"Your speech dumbfounds me. You have a marvelous, natural directness, very edifying. Perhaps I'm alone with my books too much. Or maybe it is you who is presumptuous . . ."

"Put a rag in it. Are you in or out?"

"In, by all means, Mr. Pugh."

"Now then. Let me tell you a little about Virginia. She was passionate, as you may know, about

83

conservation. When I met her, she was already terribly upset about the spraying, and had gone to Cape May County Mosquito Commission meetings to try and set them straight. Despite her bashfulness, she was determined to make a difference. It was like a new lease on life for me to meet her. I had thought I was the only one who was willing to fight.

"I gave her a stack of New Yorker magazines that contained the serialized *Silent Spring* by Rachel Carson. *Silent Spring* makes the case against pesticides virtually incontrovertible, and Virginia was sure she had found the ammunition she needed.

"Shortly before we met there had been a big fish kill—hatchling fish: menhaden, weakfish, striped bass—that covered the Creek like a silver blanket. The Mosquito Commission put out the story that it was a shortage of oxygen in the water, but Virginia had taken a couple of specimens. Now that she knew what she was looking for, she sent them away to a lab somewhere—not Rutgers, which she felt was in collusion with the chemical companies—and they found large concentrations of malathion—now that's a relatively short lived organophosphate—and she was able to ascertain that the Mosquito Commission had "treated" the area with malathion. Since organophosphates break down more quickly than the organochlorides, she knew the fish had to have come into contact with the chemical very recently. This did not go over big with the Mosquito Commission, the sprayers, politicians, anybody. And, as I say, it was this *Silent Spring* material that had given her the ammunition."

"When they really started leaning on her, even I told her to back off. She corresponded with Rachel Carson, who also advised caution, but who inspired Virginia no end. When Rudy Smick came around—he was the man with the spraying contract—to admire her art work, and even buy a piece, she was skeptical, but flattered. Later I found out through a woodsy-pig friend who had a conscience and used to spy for me that they had a big laugh about it over at the Mosquito Commission, and took turns throwing darts at the painting. On a subsequent visit, Virginia gave Smick a much chillier reception and that seemed to end their contact."

"You gettin' all this?" Jack asked me. "My head started spinning a little way back, but it snapped to attention when I heard the name of that no good Rudy Smick."

"To continue," Weston said. "This was about the time that Virginia began to get some serious, disturbing, anonymous threats. One morning she found a cryptic, typewritten warning tied around the neck of a dead animal in her boat—a muskrat, I think it was. It said something like, 'Lay off, wench. Next time this could be you.'

"It spooked her. She called me from a little pay phone in Dennisville, very shaken up. She didn't want to tell her parents, she said, because they'd forbid her to go out, and she didn't want that. She didn't have a car. She had walked to the Creek that day, though she usually cycled. At any rate, I rounded her up in my Vauxhaul—that's a small British car—and we went to my house to recover. She had some sketching materials, so after we'd had some tea, she sketched while I showed her a little bit of sculpting. That's when the idea of doing her in bronze was born. I eventually did a series of sketches, and later, when I began the sculpture, I used those when she was unable to pose for me. But I digress. In short, our time together was, in the grand scheme of things, cruelly brief. But it remains the high point of my existence.

"She got another note, sometime later, after she'd calmed down a little. This one was around the neck of a drowned cat. It said, 'Accidents happen.' 'Cowards,' she fumed. 'They don't scare me, whoever they are.' She wrote a very blistering letter to the editor—something I'd done several times—but she named names, and pulled no punches. She told about her treatment at meetings, cited those who had harassed her, and intimated collusion between government officials and private business. The paper did an investigative article on the subject, and Virginia had the idea she was really getting somewhere. But then she became the news. 'Local Birdwatcher Missing.' Then, 'Body of Missing Girl Found.' I have no doubt that it was no accident. But my relationship to her bore no value to her family, and so I was reluctant to push very hard. I still regret not doing more, and that is why, despite my reservations, I have consented to talk to you. Have you any questions?"

"We ain't got any ears left, is what we got," Jack said.

"Uh, no, not right now," I said. "But we'll stay in touch."

CHAPTER FOURTEEN

THE UNDERWOOD

Well, now I had a scoop for Lisa. I told her about my visit to Westy, what he said and all. She was impressed, said it confirmed a lot of what was in the journal, and cleared some things up. She said she'd look through the clippings and stuff in the back of the journal to see if Virginia's letters to the editor were there, or the articles the paper did about spraying and stuff. We said we'd talk later. I headed off for Andy's.

I felt like I was holding back on the old guy, what with all I now knew about his daughter, some of which I'm sure he didn't know. But I didn't see how telling him stuff at this point was going to help matters any.

"Looking like a boat, ain't she?" Andy said when we made our way back to his workshop. He had been working on the boat by himself, which was something he'd never done before. He had put on some cleats, a bow ring through the stem, and had fitted up some hardware to the spars. He had rigged up a little gizmo on the two booms so they would pivot at both ends, and put a bronze ring on the lower one so the mast could fit through it. He had fastened a pulley to the top of the mast to run the halyard through.

"Most of this stuff come off of Virginia's boat. I could use a coupla more pieces, though. If you know anybody does a lotta sailing, has boats and all, they might have some stuff around. We could use a little of this and that. Now let's varnish up these spars, and git a sail made up. I got the drawings around for it somewhere."

The boat wasn't even painted yet, and Andy wanted the spars varnished. I guess you could say he was getting pretty psyched. And I knew it meant a lot for him to give me the stuff off Virginia's boat. Now, I wondered, where does a body get a sail made? I asked Andy if he had any ideas.

"That there awning lady down in Clermont. Awnings, flags, pup tents. Goes by the name o' Dolly. Anything made with needle and thread, she can handle, believe me boy. Now, before we do that, I guess we oughtta put a couple seats on either side abaft the centerboard, and see if we can't get a rudder and tiller organized. You can take that traveler off o' the girl's boat, too, when you get a chance. Bronze don't never go bad, you notice that?"

So we still had a few more days work on the boat. It was really magnificent. In fact, I wished it was all I had to think about, but this other business was gnawing at my guts. We worked along, though, and I really got lost in the work, even when Lisa hit me with a thunderbolt when I got back from Dolly's after ordering up a sail.

"I found the notes. The death threats, I mean. And you better brace yourself. If you ask me, they were typed on Pop Berman's typewriter."

"What makes you think that?"

"You know the copy you gave me of the questions for Weston MacBride? Well, I saw this movie once, where they traced threatening notes like that to a typewriter with a dropped letter. So I looked at the notes, and right away I noticed the 'e's' were tilted back just a little bit, and the 'h' fell a little low on the line. Something about that, or just the kind of type, struck me as familiar. I looked at other typed stuff Virginia had. It didn't have those characteristics. Of course, I keep the list of questions handy, and when I looked at them you

90

could have knocked me over with a feather. It was no fluke. *All* 'e's' and 'h's' looked that way! It's almost like a fingerprint."

"Maybe all those old Underwoods did that," I suggested, without much faith.

"I very much doubt it, Joseph."

"Oh, man."

"Yeah."

Now I was really in a spot. It was hard not to suspect old Pop now. But Leon was helping me. And he was my friend, to boot. What in the world would he say if I hit him with this one? I tried to sit on it for a while, but that didn't work at all. I broke down and called Leon. I figured I'd beat around the bush a little. Maybe I could come at it sort of sideways. I had to try something.

I said the boat was just about done, so I'd like him to see it sometime. Then I told him about getting the letter back from Weston MacBride and going to his house with Jack and all. He was rather pissed at me for not telling him sooner. I felt bad, because I hadn't really thought about it.

"Call me when you're in a jam. But when you're with your other pals, oh, noo, you're too good for little pansy-face Leon."

I was surprised, because Leon's usually so, like, meek, or whatever.

"Sorry. I was just caught up in working on the boat and all ..."

He seemed to get over it by the time we hung up, but we didn't get anywhere. I decided I'd better head on over to his house and get things straightened out.

It didn't take long once I got there. It was kind of a shame, really, because he was so glad I came over that he went overboard apologizing. But still I knew he was right. We talked about different things, but before long we got to the Virginia caper. I could see that it made Leon a little uncomfortable when we talked about it this time, which it hadn't before. After awhile, when we got a little settled in up in his room, he said his Pop had been talking to him about it.

"'First,' he said, 'what happened to that Jackson girl wasn't right. I'm not at liberty to explain how I know that, but I do. It'll do no good to dig up old bones now, though.' Just like that. Then another time he asked me what you were so interested for. I said you were working with Andy Jackson, and heard about it, and were curious, that's all. He said I wasn't to mention our conversations, so I feel bad talking behind his back. But if he's hiding something—I don't know. I don't think its right. But you have to stick by me. Don't you spread it around. It might be nothing, anyway. But he made me wonder a little when he asked me if you ever said anything about Rudy Smick. I said, 'No, why?' and he just said, 'Rudy Smick's a no good S.O.B.' Maybe that's why I was a little jumpy. He is my Pop, after all."

"Yeah, I know," I said. "It sounds like he's a little troubled. Like he has suspicions, maybe. Not like he was involved or anything." There was an uneasy silence, for just 30 seconds or so.

"All right, what's up? You're acting weirder than me," Leon said.

"Nothing, why?"

"C'mon."

"No nothing. Really." I said. We paused again.

"Look," I said. "There is something. But it might be nothing. I don't know. Anyway, there were these notes. They were attached to dead animals left in Virginia's boat, two different times, not long before she died. They were typed. Virginia saved them. Lisa found them in Virginia's notebook."

"Yeah?"

"Remember the questions you typed for Weston MacBride? I compared them to the notes." (I didn't mention Lisa just yet.) "The type is the same."

"Like there weren't three million of those typewriters made."

"Wait a minute. There were two flaws that came up every time. The 'e' was tilted and the 'h' was low. It seems like a little more than a coincidence to me."

Leon looked stunned. And mad. He didn't say anything. He just glared at me.

"L-look," I said. "It doesn't mean your Pop had anything to do with it. How long has he had the typewriter? Did he ever lend it out? To Rudy Smick, maybe?"

"He's not a murderer. You Basses might not be so fond of him, but he's a good guy to me. You're supposed to be my friend."

"I am your friend. Let's forget about it."

"Yeah, let's," Leon said. But of course, neither of us could. Leaving was real uncomfortable.

CHAPTER FIFTEEN

FINISHING TOUCHES

I didn't cheer up at all until Kate told me Lisa had called to invite me out to a movie. I called her back and said something goofy like "hey, I dig this women's lib." She came by with her parents and her brother Dennis. They dropped Lisa and me off at the movies in Stone Harbor and went off miniature golfing with Dennis. Miniature golfing is something I've never done, nor had any inclination to do, so it seemed funny that two adults who could do whatever they wanted would do it voluntarily. But I guess it was a treat for Dennis. Anyway, it worked out for us.

We did a lot of whispering during the movie— catching up, going over old stuff. I didn't mention the Leon stuff, though.

When Lisa found out how far along I was on the boat, she said, "Let's get together and work on painting it up," and maybe she could exchange the journal for another one (minus the threatening notes) while we were at it.

As it turned out, the next day was a day off for Kate, and all three of us went over to Andy's to look things over. We asked Andy whether it was time to paint the boat, since we'd gotten the paint and all.

When we realized we didn't have any brushes, Andy sent us back to the old sign painter's.

"Old Enscoe's got hundreds of them. Real good ones. I used to borrow them and bring 'em back none the worse for the wear. He gets extra good quality ones. You could never afford them, nor would you be likely to use them again.

So over we went. He was, according to Kate, "another old eccentric." It was funny how different he was when I went over with the two girls instead of Jack. He was just real low key, pleasant. A little bashful, almost. He gave us about 10 different brushes, enough to paint five or six boats—along with advice on thinning the paint properly, brushing it on properly, care of brushes, etc. He gave us strict instructions on their care. He had hundreds of them in buckets, just as Andy had said, their bristles wrapped in paper, soaking in dirty looking gasoline and turpentine.

Of the colors we had gotten on our first visit we decided on off white for the hull, buff for the topsides, and just linseed oil and thinner for the interior part. That's just about exactly how Virginia's boat had been painted, we realized. Andy had a heavy hand in choosing the colors, and said, when we were done, "now that could just be little Ginny's boat. If I could only step back in time, everything'd be perfect."

He got a little misty eyed, and Kate went and put her arm around his shoulder. He looked little next to her. She was actually a little taller, and he was so skinny and saggy looking. He patted her hand and said, "this ain't so bad, though. But I ain't anxious for the sail to get done. I'll be sorry to see her go."

"Well, we still have to get the bottom paint," I said, helpfully.

"You won't be sorry if we take you down to the Creek, and Joe gives you a ride in her, will you?"

"I reckon not," he said, his eyes twinkling. "Now you youngsters come into the house. I got something to show you."

We went in, and he pulled out his "secret drawer" from under his kitchen table, the one he kept his money in. He pulled out a framed 8"x10" photograph and laid it on the table.

"Her friend MacBride took it," he said.

Nobody said a word. There was a pretty little sailboat, up on sawhorses. In front of it stood a beautiful black haired girl. She had a big, broad smile on her face. And she had her arm around a muscular, ruggedly built, slightly familiar looking man. After a few seconds I realized it must be Andy, all those years ago. The boat was the spitting image of mine, except that it had the name "Rachel" lettered neatly on the side.

"The Rachel, is what she called it. After Rachel Carson. Enscoe put them letters on there. He was just a young man then. He bartered the job. She took him for a sail. The feller would'a lettered everything on the place if she'd 'a kept taking him. He was that smitten, you see. But not Virginia's type, apparently."

After we left, Kate said to me: "Who does she remind you of? Virginia, I mean."

97

"I don't know, ah, Cindy, maybe?"

"Yeah. Spitting image, I think." Lisa wasn't especially interested in this line of conversation, I could tell.

"Yeah, so she does," I said, realizing I'd seen them both, if you consider the sculpture, in almost the same attire, as you might say.

"It's kind of spooky," Kate went on. "Speaking of which, once you get the sail made, I bet Cindy'd come over and help you get the bugs worked out, sailing wise, I mean."

"I'm sure she would," Lisa piped up. Kate and I just kind of smirked to ourselves.

* * *

That evening I got a surprise visit from Leon. Any visit from Leon is a surprise, because he gets out so rarely. We went out in the yard, and he said we'd better talk about his Pop and all.

"I can't just ignore it," he said. "It's eating me up inside. If he's not involved, it's not right to have these suspicions. And if he is involved—well, that's just a chance I'll have to take. But somehow we've got to get to the bottom of it. For everybody's sake."

"I guess you're right," I said. "I had kind of put it aside. But it's been bothering me, too. What do you have in mind?"

"I don't know, exactly. Somehow we've got to get him to talk. That won't be easy to do. Did you ever notice how he takes a ride almost every evening? About eight o'clock or so. I think he rides down to Mosquito Point and looks out over the marshes. That's what Granny says. And drinks highballs. He always takes his 'hot 'n cooler' with the ginger ale. 'Brings back fond memories,' Granny says. I'm not so sure. Something tells me that whatever's eating him, he goes out there and drowns his sorrows. He does it more nowadays, and he's been a lot moodier lately. I might be reading too much into it, but I don't think so. I think the answer is out there somewhere, if we could just figure out the puzzle."

"I'll think on it, Leon. Is it all right if I talk to Jack or Lisa about it, to see if they have any ideas?"

"Man, I don't know. Use your judgment, I guess. I trust you. We've got to come up with something."

* * *

"What's up with Leon?" Kate asked me when I went into the house. "He looked like he had the future of civilization riding on him. Now you look a little bit like that yourself."

"Can you keep a secret?" I asked. She said yes, so I laid it all out for her. She knew some of the story, but of course not the new stuff about Pop Berman. I figured she was as likely as anybody to have an idea. More likely, maybe.

"Pop Berman is not the most popular guy in the world," Kate said. "But implicating him in a murder is pretty strong stuff."

"I'm not saying he did it. I'm saying he might know something about it," I said.

"Or he might be involved," Kate added.

"Yeah, maybe."

"Well, if he hasn't talked yet, he's not likely to," Kate said. "Did it ever occur to you that he just thinks it's impertinent for you and Leon to be probing around, and that he has absolutely no connection at all to the thing, except having found the body? Don't you think that would be upsetting enough for the guy, so that he wouldn't be all that enthusiastic about discussing the subject?"

"We thought of that, but the business about the typewriter seems pretty conclusive, wouldn't you say?"

"Maybe he bought it from a yard sale. O.K. It doesn't look good, I have to admit. I'm just playing devil's advocate. I have to admit it's awful suspicious, especially in light of Pop's connection to the Mosquito Commission and all. And being tied up with Rudy Smick. Like you say, he seems to be very troubled about it, conflicted. There must be some way to get him talking."

"Maybe when he's down at Mosquito Point, with a few highballs in him, he might loosen up," I said jokingly.

"Maybe you're not such a dope after all," Kate said. "You know that saying '*in vino veritas*?' It means that wine, in sufficient portions, brings out the truth."

"Then why does Dad say that bars are places where men who don't actually accomplish much go to get drunk and tell lies?"

"Maybe they're drinking beer," Kate laughed. "But listen to this. You know how much Cindy looks like those pictures of Virginia, and she's such a good sailor? How about if old Pop Berman was sitting in his car, feeling drunk and sentimental, right around twilight, and the ghost of Virginia Jackson sailed by on her boat. You think that might shock him into loosening up his tongue?"

"It's pretty far fetched. And who would be there to listen to him? Would we bug his car?"

"I don't know. It is far fetched. But that doesn't necessarily make it bad. The light bulb was far fetched when Thomas Edison first thought of it."

"It's got some good points, but it needs a little more. I mean, I like it and all, but if it had just a little more punch, a little more shock value."

* * * *

The next day I told Leon about Kate's idea. He thought it sounded interesting, but hard to pull off. And he was against bugging Pop's car. Lisa liked it, except for the part about Cindy.

101

I went over to Andy's, and we put some finishing touches on the boat. I had picked up some bottom paint, and Dolly had called to say the sail was done. Kate and I went over to pick it up later that day, and I'd say Dolly didn't charge enough. It was really a spectacular looking thing, all laid out on her huge sewing table. She even made a sail bag from some scraps of striped canvas, which we put the sail in after we had folded it up. We then went around and rounded up Cindy, who Kate had already talked to, and she brought along a bucket of miscellaneous pulleys, clips, cleats and such rigging goodies, along with some neatly coiled sheets and halyards.

On the ride out to Andy's, Kate gave Cindy a brief summary of the situation and then explained our idea of her posing as Virginia, since she looked so much like her and was the only person we knew who could sail like her. Cindy thought it sounded like a blast.

We rigged up the boat, and "dry-sailed" it there in the yard. I told Andy he'd get the first ride, once Cindy'd worked all the kinks out.

"If Cindy, here, is at the helm, I'll totter on board somehow," he chuckled. "But if it means you'll keep bringing around these bewitching beauties, that make an old sack o' bones feel like a boy again, I might just chain the skiff to a tree here, to keep you coming back."

"Don't worry, Andy," Kate said. "I'm sure this isn't Joe's last boat-building project. He thinks about boats and draws little sketches of boats and talks about boats pretty much around the clock. I'm sure you'll see plenty of him."

CHAPTER SIXTEEN

THE RACHEL RIDES AGAIN

I told Lisa that night that we were just about ready to launch the boat.

"You mean the 'Rachel,'" she said. "Better get that old sign painter to letter her up like the original, if we want our scheme to work." We arranged for Lisa to come down the next day for the big launching.

We hooked up my dad's utility trailer to the Suburban, and Dad, Kate and I drove over to Andy's. We hossed the boat up on the trailer and tied it down, and I helped Andy into the car. Then we putted over to Enscoe's shop. He admired the boat from every angle, got out a brush and lettered "Rachel" on the sides exactly as he'd lettered Virginia's boat so many years before, and refused to take anything for his services.

When we got back to our house, Lisa was there along with her dad and her little brother Dennis. They were talking to Cindy, who had come over for the shakedown cruise. Lisa and Cindy piled into the Suburban, and Dennis and Mr. Ronson followed in his pickup as we headed down to the creek.

There is a little slipway not far from the rickety little dock I used to tie my old, dry-rotted garvey to. We backed up to it, and everybody got a hold of the boat along its two sides, and we slid it in. I had a long painter hitched to the bow cleat, and I let the boat drift on out

into the creek. It looked magnificent. Just a simple little
skiff. But, like Kate said, it looked so elegant.

Andy and I were so puffed up we could hardly stand up right. After a while Cindy came over and took the painter from me and pulled the boat back in. She climbed aboard, stepped the mast and got everything rigged up. It broke the spell a little when she slipped on the paddle that was laying in the bottom and took a slightly ungainly spill. Then she pushed off with the paddle, pulled the sheet in and sailed away down the Creek.

She didn't go far, jibing and tacking back and forth in front of us. Then, as she pulled up to the rickety dock, she dropped the sail just in time to glide to a stop.

"Andy's first," she said.

"I feel like I'm seeing a bee-uteeful ghost," Andy said. "Don't she just put me in mind of my little girl." He was climbing stiffly aboard when a sporty little car pulled up. We all turned, and saw Jack get out of the passenger side.

"Age before beauty, I see," Jack said as he looked at Andy getting in the boat. "That means I'm next."

Out of the driver's side came a flashy looking brunette in her late twenties or so.

"Oh," Jack croaked. "I'd like you to meet my fiancee. Stephanie. I ain't popped the question yet, but as you can see she's crazy about me."

"Hi, I'm Cindy's sister. Nothing's final yet about our plans, but can you blame me for being interested? He even has his own plane." She seemed like a very good sport.

106

We all stood and watched Cindy go up, back and around with Andy beaming the whole time.

We all got rides eventually, and I even found I could sail, after a fashion. My lesson hadn't been a total loss. Stephanie and Jack only stayed a few minutes. She had been up checking out Jack's plane, and now they were heading out to Woodbine to go up in a 140 Cessna Stephanie was thinking of buying.

"The 140 is cute," she said as they left. "But Jack's big old Stearman has stolen my heart."

My dad, Lisa, Kate, Andy and I piled into the Suburban. Cindy headed for home, and so did Mr. Ronson and Dennis. On the way to our house, we dropped Andy off. He was in pretty high spirits, but it was sad watching him shuffle into his little house all alone as we pulled away.

We got home, and after my dad went into the house, Lisa, Kate and I sat down and mapped out our strategy. I called Leon on the shop phone, and we arranged for him to come over on his bike that evening, as soon as his Pop went out to have his highballs.

I was jittery for the rest of the day. Lisa didn't seem perturbed at all. She was staying for dinner, which meshed with our plans. I couldn't help thinking that we needed just a little more to get Pop talking. The sailboat might be enough, I could see that, but what if it wasn't? I still had butterflies during dinner. But everyone acted real natural when Cindy stopped by afterwards. She didn't pay much attention to Lisa and me, just hung out with Kate. We walked outside while they gabbed, and before long Leon rolled in on his bike. Then in another minute, my friend Freddy rolled up on his bike.

"Does he know?" Leon asked.

Freddy looked put out to have been excluded, whatever was going on.

"Might as well bring him up to speed," Leon said. So we gave him a rough outline of our plan and where we stood.

Kate and Cindy came outside. Kate said she had asked Mom if she could take all us kids down to see the boat in the Suburban and maybe get some ice cream on the way.

"All right, here's the deal," Kate said. "Everybody in, and we'll give final instructions while we're driving. Joe and Leon, put your bikes in the back. Freddy, you'll be working with Lisa and me. Cindy, do you have your Virginia outfit?"

"Right in my car. Just a sec."

I noticed Kate had put three handheld VHF radios in the car. When I asked what they were for, she said they were for her and Cindy to be able to communicate, in case she got hung up somewhere, and one extra in case we needed a sentinel somewhere.

"Do Mom and Dad know anything about this?" I asked.

"Of course not. They'd think we were crazy."

"So you snuck Dad's VHF's?"

"Nothing will happen to them, Mr. Boy Scout."

Kate was in rare form. She was supposed to be the goody-two shoes. Maybe it was because her friend was there. Or maybe she was just really into it. Whatever it was, I was actually glad to see her so fired up. It made the whole project seem more likely to succeed.

We dropped Cindy, Lisa and Freddy off at the Creek landing, with two of the radios. Then we drove to Mosquito Point Road. Just where the woods stop and the open marshes begin, we stopped and got our bikes out. We mounted up just around a little curve, so we wouldn't be noticed in Pop's rear view mirror. The road across the marshes out to the landing was arrow straight, and we didn't really want him to see the Suburban either, so Kate backed up and parked in the shadows.

We were both feeling nervous, or at least I felt it and Leon sure looked it, as we pedaled out along the pitted gravel road. It's real pretty and marsh smelly along there. A lot of birds like herons and terns were hanging around. It seemed so peaceful I was starting to have second thoughts about the trap we were setting. But I also had the feeling Pop might not be especially affected by the sight of the girl in the boat. Of course, I had my doubts about whether seeing the girl in the boat would jar him enough to spill his guts anyway, but that was our plan, and we were stuck with it.

When we got to the car Pop looked very surprised to see us.

109

"Gran said it was all right to take a ride, Pop," Leon said quickly, sounding worried.

"It's a hell of a ways from home, Leon." We sat there on our bikes for a few minutes, while Pop looked straight ahead.

"What are you looking at, Pop?" Leon asked. Pop looked a little dazed. Drunk, I guess. He didn't say anything.

"Joe's alright," Pop said after a while, almost as if I wasn't there. "Hisolman's alright too," he said, a little slurred-like. Leon looked embarrassed. "You boys want some ginger ale?" he said after another pause. "Get in. I'll move the cooler. No whiskey in your drinks, though." He smiled a tiny bit, and seemed to be concentrating, aware, maybe, that Leon was embarrassed about his high-ball thickened tongue. He lifted the hot 'n cooler off the front seat and set it on the floor of the back. He always kept the back seat of his station wagon folded down so it was more like a panel truck. Leon slid into the middle of the seat then I got in. Pop put his hand on Leon's knee.

"Doesn't hurt for you t' get out and see the world a little. Joe's a little rough around the edges, but he's a good boy," he said slowly. "You gotta mix it up a little. Exper-i-ence, ah life." Then he fell into silence, and we all just looked straight ahead.

"I've been a bastard in some ways, not real popular, boy. But I always looked after the family. You wouldn't be any better off as a poor orphan, except it might toughen

110

you up a little. The ladies don't mean to be so protective, but everybody always felt so bad for you, we didn't want you to suffer any more."

"I know, Pop." Leon said. I noticed a sail poking up over to the marshes off to the left. Pop and Leon didn't seem to notice it yet. Pop was into one of his glazed silences, and Leon was a little misty-eyed. As the sail came closer, Leon noticed it and looked over at me. It was almost in front of us, just a little to the left still, when Pop turned to take it in.

"She's back!" he said. "No, I'm seeing things." He kept staring at the boat. His chin started quivering, like he was cold.

"M-maybe she's not dead. No. It was over 20 years ago. I saw her. All bloated. But look."

"What are you talking about, Pop?" Leon said. "Who's not dead?" But Pop didn't answer. He just watched the skiff sail away around the bend. You could still see the top of the sail above the marshes. For a minute I forgot it was my boat, and thought it was Virginia come back to life.

"Did you see the name on that boat, boy?" Pop asked.

"Yeah, Pop, it said 'Rachel' on the side."

"What the Hell's going on here. Are you boys up to something?"

"No," Leon said. "Up to what? What are you talking about?" Just then the boat came back into view—she had come about and was heading back towards us.

"Nobody can sail a boat like that around here," Pop said, "'cept the Jackson girl. She could sail up a drainage ditch into a headwind, is what they used to say about her."

I began to notice the drone of an airplane. It was getting loud enough to be annoying, and it seemed to have a familiar, low throb to it. Pop looked around, real concerned. Then, just as the boat was almost in front of us, a big yellow biplane swooped down from behind us and seemed to almost touch the mast of the boat. The roar was deafening as it climbed back up into the sky. It looped around like it was going to make another pass.

"No, No, No! Smick! You Bastard!" Pop was hollering as he got out of the car. We got out, too. The plane came back and swooped down lengthwise with the creek, buzzing the boat again, whipping the sail up and even frothing the water a little. Cindy flopped over the side into the water. There was smoke coming out of the back of the plane. Pop, who was down on his knees and ducking, got up and charged into the water after her. Leon and I ran after him and hauled him back up the bank, one of us on each shoulder. He was a strong old guy. He was blubbering and crying and covered with mud, and he had lost his glasses.

"It was Smick," he was saying. "That no good S.O.B. Rudy Smick. I covered for him. I knew he did it. He was just trying to scare her, he said, and to prove that the spray wasn't harmful. But it was. She went overboard and drowned. Smick told me. And I didn't say anything. Other people helped Rudy cover it up, too.

112

I don't know exactly who. But I figured it wouldn't do those Jacksons any good to find out. Nobody could bring her back. I come out here in the evenings and think about what I've done . . ."

Cindy, who'd had a hold of a rope tied to the skiff when she went over, had gotten back aboard and sailed over to us. She hopped out, soaking wet, and pulled the bow up onto the bank.

"That Stephanie can really fly a plane, can't she? Did you see Jack in there, running the smoker?" Cindy said, excitedly.

"You alright, mister?" she asked, kneeling down and patting Pop on the shoulder like you might to an upset little kid. Pop was sitting on the bank, his legs down the slope, his feet in the muddy water.

"You set me up, son," he said to Leon. Leon looked sick.

"You could've told the truth," Leon said, finally. "What was I supposed to do? When I found out stuff about it, I couldn't just pretend I hadn't. I couldn't unlearn it. Why'd you do it, Pop? Why?"

"You're right, boy. I could have told the truth. Now I've hurt you with this scandal, and protected Rudy Smick. It should have been the other way around. Maybe I can undo some of the damage by setting things aright," Pop said, struggling to his feet. Leon stood right next to Pop, and Pop put his arm around Leon. "I guess this friend of yours is not such a bad influence after all,"

113

he said, and pulled me over towards him with his other hand and clapped me on the back.

"Rudy Smick is in for the surprise of his life," Pop said as the Suburban rolled up behind us. Kate, Freddy, and Lisa hopped out.

"I went back and got them from the landing," Kate said. "They called me on the VHF and said the mosquitoes were eating them alive. We almost missed the whole thing."

"Who's not in on this?" Pop said.

"The police, for one," Lisa volunteered.

"How come we weren't let in on the airplane part," I asked, feeling kind of put out.

"We wanted you and Leon to be as surprised as Pop," Lisa said.

"Thanks a million," I said back, not too thrilled.

"Pop," Leon said. "I think there's an old guy who deserves an explanation. Do you feel up to it?"

"No. I don't feel up to much of anything. But I guess that's what I've gotta do. To think all you kids, and even Jack Pugh, were in on this thing." He sounded rather more bad tempered now. "To think you all believed I was no good, that I was a liar. Did anyone stick up for me at all?"

"Leon did," I said. "He was ready to rip my lungs out when I said I thought you were in on it, that your typewriter matched the threatening notes."

"What notes? The ones Rudy typed on my Underwood? I never read them; I just let him use the typewrighter."

"Anyway, Leon stuck up for you," I repeated.

"And I guess I was wrong, wasn't I Pop?"

"Yeah. I guess you were. But not for sticking up for me. Just on the facts." They walked back toward the car together, Pop's arm on Leon's shoulder. After a few steps Leon put his arm around Pop's waist.

I looked around and noticed tears on a couple of people's faces. But it was hard to see exactly, my eyes being a little blurry themselves.

"I guess Virginia can rest easy, now," Kate said.

We weren't all jubilant at our success, like I expected we'd be.

Cindy and Freddy got into the boat and sailed back toward our landing. The rest of us got into the Suburban and headed to the same place. There wasn't much conversation, but we all felt relieved, I'm sure of that.